A BOOK, UNTITLED

TRANSLATED BY

A BOOK, UNTITLED

SHUSHAN AVAGYAN

DEANNA
CACHOIAN-SCHANZ

TILTED AXIS PRESS

CONTENTS

A NOTE ON *BOOK* AND ITS
HISTORICAL PROTAGONISTS
FROM THE TRANSLATOR

Girq-anvernagir was published as samizdat in Yerevan in 2006. The book's cover image—two black, empty cast iron chairs seated on opposite sides of a matching black table, set slightly to the left—meets the eye against a minimalist red and white backdrop, setting the stage for an unassuming 128 pages divided into 26.5 chapters composed in Eastern Armenian.

Written as a literary experiment while its author was simultaneously translating the poems of Armenian writer Shushanik Kurghinian into English, *Girq-anvernagir* reads on its surface as a translator's diary. However, through seemingly unrelated and fragmented vignettes in disparate and unidentified voices, the reader discovers that Avagyan is actually mapping out a larger archival or archeological site. The book's first chapter, "Preface, or We as Two Separate Planets," draws our map: an imagined encounter between two early twentieth-century writers, Shushanik Kurghinian and Zabel Yesayan, whose legacies have largely been obscured and forgotten. Juxtaposed with this fictive meeting is a conversation between two characters—"the typist/writer" (ostensibly Avagyan, the author) and her friend Lara—who share with each other what they've uncovered while sifting through the archives of various state institutions in Yerevan in their effort to piece together the forgotten stories of Kurghinian and Yesayan. The novel opens with "the typist/writer" and Lara sitting in a café in Yerevan, just as their predecessors might have done. Discussing the fragments they have found in the archive, including letters that were written to the forgotten authors, the friends are burdened with questions of loss. Lara suggests to write a book about it. Avagyan answers her call.

In the chapters that unfold, *Girq-anvernagir* not only tells the story of the author and her friend's search for Kurghinian and Yesayan, but through that story, the novel is also a poetic reflection on authorship and the fashioning of the self. The novel, then, might best be described as a work of metafiction or autotheory—a genre of literature in which the text theorizes itself. As such, *A Book, Untitled* tells a story about, in, and through archival gaps: an approach through which Avagyan as author and literary critic offers her own commentary on censorship, editorship, translation, and the lost legacies of these (women) authors in the Armenian literary and historical canons.

The main historical protagonists of *A Book, Untitled* are the authors Shushanik Kurghinian and Zabel Yesayan. Shushanik Kurghinian (1876–1927) was a poetry and prose writer from Alexandrapol (present-day Gyumri, Armenia) who wrote highly revolutionary poetry, women's rights central to her voice. Kurghinian (née Popoljian) attended primary school at a local monastery, then the Alexandrapol Arghutian Girls' School, and later a Russian gymnasium. Kurghinian was the founder of the first women's branch of the Social Democrat Hunchakian Party in her hometown. In 1897, she married Arshak Kurghinian, who was a member of the socialist underground in the Caucasus. In 1903, under the threat of ending up in the Tsar's Siberia after being blacklisted and set to be arrested for her socialist activism in Alexandrapol, she escaped with her two children, Arshakanoush and Shavarsh, to Rostov-on-Don. Her third child, Arsham, was born in 1910. Kurghinan remained in Rostov with the children while Arshak returned to Alexandrapol to tend to the family business. Kurghinian returned to Armenia in 1921, when the country became a socialist republic, at the invitation of Alexander Miasnikian, the Chairman of the Council of People's Commissars of Armenia (1921–1922). As a poet, Kurghinian was criticized both by the tsarist regime and Armenian writers and nationalist members of the Armenian Revolutionary Federation (or Dashnaktsutyun Party) for her socialist and revolutionary ideas. Despising her socialist themes and unable or unwilling to acknowledge the strength of her writing, they criticized Kurghinian for her lack of "artistry." Later, in the Soviet era, her overtly feminist poems were ignored, while her poems devoted to the working class were used to serve the ruling political opportunisms of the Soviet party and its ideology. After the collapse of the Soviet Union, even as a proletarian poet, Kurghinian was simply forgotten. Her name remained only in the memories of the older generation—a trace of Soviet propaganda.

Zabel Yesayan (1878–1943?) was a prose writer, translator, and literature professor from Constantinople (present-day Istanbul, Turkey). She was a prolific writer, whose early works depicted a multiculturalist Ottoman society, giving voice to characters across ethnoreligious divides as well as denouncing social conservatism. At a young age, Yesayan (née Hovhannesian) was sent to study at a neighborhood school in her native city, and later, attended classes in Paris, including at the Sorbonne. She married the painter Dikran Yesayan in 1900 while in Paris, and in 1901, their daughter Sophie was born.

For extended periods following, their family both migrated together and was separated: Yesayan moved back and forth from Paris to Constantinople between 1902 and 1908, finally resettling in Constantinople following the Young Turk Revolution. Her son Hrant was born in 1910, in Paris, during yet another sojourn. After continued back and forth between the two cities, Dikran took Sophie and moved definitively to Paris. Yesayan and Hrant remained in Constantinople. Yesayan fled Constantinople to Bulgaria in the fall of 1915 to escape persecution: she was one of those listed on the April 24 Blacklist of 1915, which condemned most of her male intellectual peers to death at the onset of the Armenian Genocide. From Bulgaria she fled to the Caucasus, where she worked with Armenian refugees, documenting their eyewitness accounts of atrocities, and from where she led relief efforts for Armenian orphans. The family was eventually reunited in France after the war in 1919. Dikran died there two years later. Yesayan made her first visit to Soviet Armenia in 1926, settling there with her two children in 1933. Four years later, she was accused of Armenian nationalism during the Great Purge in 1937. She was first imprisoned and then physically disposed of by the Stalin regime sometime around 1943. The details and location of her disappearance have been censored. Later, the majority of her seminal literary works were hardly popular. Yesayan is the author of sixteen works, including novels and essays written in Armenian, French, and Turkish. Kurghinian is derided and forgotten; Yesayan is killed. Yet, in 1926, the year in which Avagyan sets their meeting, the lives of both women overlap in Yerevan: Yesayan has just arrived in the Soviet Armenian capital, and Kurghinian dies there one year later, in 1927.

"Literature is a weapon to struggle against injustice," wrote Zabel Yesayan. In Avagyan's contemporary response to the literary canon's erasure of Kurghinian and Yesayan, *Girq* takes Yesayan's task to arms by formally mimicking the very erasure and distortion of the canon that it criticizes. *Girq* autocensors through the use of ****, plagiarizes poetry and prose (from Kurghinian, Yesayan, and elsewhere), and uncovers lost h(er)stories. In so doing, *Girq* performs various forms of censorship and provokes the question of "who can author?"

As the novel progresses, it becomes apparent that the "typist/writer" is also writing love postcards, the lines of which pepper the novel in *italics*. Who is the recipient of these unaddressed postcards? A lover, the writers, the reader, a homeland? Who is the speaker? What is historical, what is imagined? Is there a difference? What has been, and what is still being censored?

Thus, through a series of meta critiques, a stream of (fictional?) memories, and this collection of unsent or unarrived love postcards (not unlike the postcards written to and by Yesayan while she was in jail), the novel, between theory and practice, recounts the story of a constant becoming. In turn, Avagyan beseeches her readers to sit in the uncomfortable knowing that neither history, nor memory, nor ourselves, are ever fully recoverable. Instead, as the novel suggests, it is our duty to re-make them, each time re-remembered, and again anew.

—D. Cachoian-Schanz

For Varanda

1. PREFACE, OR WE AS
TWO SEPARATE PLANETS

Dear Marina Tsvetaeva, I wish you hadn't hurried. I'm standing below your window now repeating your words: When you love, you live without Hope.

In spring.

The next time we met, she told me not to write her anymore.

Starting today, she said.

One day in spring.

On March 22 of 1960, Sophie Yesayan writes, "My mother was in the city jail; I needed to see her. She caressed my two-year-old child and said to her, 'You'll be a pioneer, and you'll say: My grandmother was a counter-revolutionary.' She asked for embroidery thread."

I am not to write to you.

Lara and I are sitting at the café on Abovyan Street, across from the museum.

Perhaps write a book (and start from the end)?

.Kurghinian's to close very philosophically were ideas her, revolutionary-counter a Though

I promise not to wait for your call, my dear.

Just imagine if they'd met each other, says Lara.

Like You and Me.

"In the Waiting Room."

Someone will remember the disappeared, and while remembering, write verses dedicated to them, and while reading those verses, yet another will re-remember them.

The loss of one thing will help re-find another.

In his letter Arshak writes, "You're torturing me. If you doubt it then take a good hard look at me." It was May 24, 1895, when the cherry blossoms had already fallen from the trees.

I'm going to write to you in an Other language so that you won't understand the underflowing current of my feelings.

In early spring, when the snow melts . . .

Some of the final pages of *Barpa Khachik* are missing.

Or more precisely, the book wasn't finished.

"Spouses are actors who simultaneously play different roles upon the same stage."

We'll reflect upon this theme in the coming chapters.

Perhaps they would have sat just like us, in a café, people-watching. One would have recounted her exiled life in Paris, and the other her life in Rostov-on-Don.

I'm dedicating this book to you.

My dear, it's been a whole week since we've seen each other. Last Sunday when you came to visit me . . .

You're the city in which I'm exiled.

Not all postcards bear such pleasant news.

Sophie writes, "I saw her twice in the summer of 1940. She said that she appealed to Beria, and now she's waiting . . . hoping for the best."

Tell me about your cocooned life, about how you were covered in silken threads, about how you fell asleep. Tell me about how your body changed colors, about how you didn't recognize yourself when you awoke, and about how the rays of the sun newly welcomed your waking eyes.

Unpublished note: "Easily possessed desire has no charm."

All the promises, all the now-and-forever-and-evers, *all of them* are irrevocable.

On one of your sidewalks, my dear, I hid a sickly seed, a tiny black-eyed seedling. Let me water it so it doesn't die.

She was writing by candlelight . . . erasing and writing: "And so, departing from your side, oh so suddenly, I will fly like lightning, and then fall back to the black earth's frigid arms, crushed by your unknowing heart."

Her first poem poured out from her with ease (like the salty waters of the Black Sea), (with the righteousness of a martyr) swooping down unashamed, unexpected, and drunken like the seagulls.

> I'll enter my office, lock my doors,
>   and turn on (Tamar's) lamp,
> My hands will take this very same pen and I'll write . . .
> Two days is an eternity
> On the frozen petals of the iris
> And I'll write: two years is old age, resting on my shoulders
>   like a wedding veil;
> And I'll write: two centuries is an ephemeral second, quivering
>   on my lips from your kiss;
> And when finally the ink of my pen dries,
> I will open my doors to the Ringing of the Dawn;
>   I'll step outside,
> Holding the pages of your life to my chest.

If we could have recovered all of the pages that had been torn out, burned, and destroyed by the critics, the libraries would simply overflow.

(let me lick all your wounds);
I descend from the tribe of the Arlez, Semiramis's immortal
    dogs,
A servant of the altar, daughter of insolence; I came
    to give you new breath, your veins new blood;
You've become lifeless, bloodless, without shelter, abandoned
    and hardened after the battle, your pride wounded . . .

Let me plant my roots in you, my city. I'll sprout and grow with new branches, and spread my roots deeper inside you.

"The warden turned down the third meeting."

One day you'll write, Lara. Just don't put it off.

The most important part of a book is its footnotes, but many people ignore them. We've got to come up with a different method.

Fifty-nine handwritten notebooks.

All the poems included in these pages (with the exception of those highlighted in the footnotes) are being published for the first time.

Sophie writes, "And just like that, I never saw my mother again."

You probably don't remember me. I always sat in the very back of the classroom, usually silent.

What should I write about? How should the book attract you, seduce you so that you don't put it down, so you can feel the hopelessness of my sleepless nights?

Only on two conditions, you said: not to write you and not to look for you.

Imagine that you're reading four books in four different languages, simultaneously.

Your hands, your strong arms, your slender, delicate fingers.

"Sometime between 1940–41 they transferred my mother from Yerevan to Leninakan," Sophie writes. "My brother saw her in prison."

Together, Lara and I went to the museum to see the manuscripts.

Sophie writes, "That was my brother's last meeting with her."

How can I trust you? How can I know? Perhaps this is also our last meeting.

Don't assume, don't wait, don't

Marina's light has faded. She's standing in the dark by the window, smoking her Gitanes cigarettes. The rings of smoke are black and envelop her body.

. . . they are collected in one generic notebook that contains about one hundred and twenty poems, both published and unpublished.

The notebook is dated: 1894–1908.

One day it'll happen: with the clarity of a lake, my mind afresh and my fingers nimble, in my own words, one day I'll write.

But now I can't—you forbid it.

These words grew on your streets, numb from your frigidity and veiled in the shadows, hidden in the cracks of the asphalt warped from the cold.

Sophie writes, "In 1939 she'd often send us postcards," embroidered with red thread.

One is preserved in the museum.

Condemned postcards.

"From 1940–41, the postcards became fewer and farther between."

A meeting that never took place.

Maybe she'd have talked about her childhood and how her father had decided to send her off to a convent, and how one day they'd locked her up in the "rodent pit" because she'd misbehaved.

It's already late, but wait just a little bit longer.

Sophie writes, "Between 1941–42, the postcards stopped." Then she adds, "I imagine she died sometime in those years."

A book composed of postcards from death row.

Sitting together in the café, they've completely forgotten that it's getting cold and that their glasses have long been empty.

"According to the official data, my mother has been sent from Yerevan to Baku," writes Sophie.

"And then from Baku to Karaganda, but she hasn't arrived. She's been placed in the unknown category."

Busts of all the beloved figures are arranged in the lobby of the state university. "But where is she?" asks Lara. "Why isn't her bust there?"

I answer.

Fifty-nine pages are missing from the book and while reading you come across asterisks denoting that some things from that section have been erased.

Sophie writes, "The Public Court withdrew her official date of death. The Registry Office dated it 1937."

It's today: men and women have gathered at the sacrificial altar.

> I surrender my possessions to you all—all of me—
>   my only dowry and riddle;
> take out my eyes, take them out with the branches of an apple
>   tree,
> place them on your silver sacrificial tray, let them dry;

henna-painted, break my fingers one-by-one
so that I won't write anymore, won't bleed from the wounds
　　of a needle;
they weren't created for embroidering;

cut off my breasts, that hang like two lovesick earrings,
they're *not* giving milk, worthless! worthless!
full of lies and maggots,
villainous! oh! villainous!

remove my tongue so I won't pray,
so that I won't sing for you in the foreign words of the
　　mythical Arlez;
this tongue, that for many lives, has been imprisoned between
　　my teeth—
silenced from fear, silenced! silenced!

Sophie writes, "I would have wanted the ashes to have been brought to our pantheon; she loved her fatherland, her compatriots; that would have been her final resting place, 'At the foot of Ararat,' as she'd liked to say."

Cause of death: unknown.

Place of death: unknown.

Brave people have formed a line all the way up to the front of the coffee shop at Logan Airport.

They make everyone remove their belts.

Her last name in Turkish means garden.

We still have two hours before the flight.

I read couplet by couplet while they compared the translation to the original.

When the three of us arrived and knocked on the door, she met us barefoot and we stood on the porch for half an hour.

It turns out the neighbors had the keys.

In his preface, Boccaccio writes on behalf of women: "Remember, we are all women and no one among us so young that she doesn't know what follies we'd make without the help of some man."

That evening we decided to go to a tearoom to get to know each other, and then begin our work the next day.

The ocean wasn't as "big" or "monstrous" as I'd imagined.

One shouldn't assume anything.

Her husband wrote letters to her almost every day: "I know that living with me is unbearable for you . . . I don't exist for you any longer . . . the differences between us have become so vast."

The very same text changes in other languages. Like a nomadic tribe, it mimics the peculiarities of the new environment and reality.

Standing by the door, the four of us got wrapped up in conversation.

They're from Zangezur, made from pieces of old buttons.

According to Lev Nikolaevich, a novel shouldn't end but begin with a marriage, since the plot should develop around its disintegration.

There was the smell of naphthalene in the house: the windows had been tightly sealed over the winter months.

Birds that don't migrate to warmer climates feel the warmth of the sun. They begin to chirp differently. They sit differently on the branches.

It's important to free oneself of the Anna Karenina syndrome.

"By nature fickle, we are all stubborn, suspicious, cowardly, and timorous, which fine qualities, I am sure, would cause us to break up our company sooner than we expected, and with little honor to ourselves, unless we had someone else to guide us," wrote Boccaccio.

I woke up at night with an irregular heart beat: the manuscript of translated poems loomed before me, and Decisions hung over it in the air like a guillotine.

This word doesn't work in this line.

One of us was married, one of us engaged, one of us single, and one of us an Amazon.

We went to Gyumri to find the house where she was born, and while her poet-friends stood on bronze pedestals, with vines of ivy adorning the entrances of their houses, hers . . .

I'm telling Tina Bastajian about this at the airport as the deafening sound of the coffee machine cuts me off.

The concept of marriage had to fail sooner or later: the future belongs to New Forms of Communal Existence, a sort of nomadic tribal life.

The house was quite dusty.

The four of us gathered in the living room the next morning.

The future belongs to those who know more than just their mother tongue and who live in apartments built of glass.

We leave the coffee shop and join the tired masses.

I believe an old Greek philosopher once said: He is laughable who speaks on behalf of others.

Seek guidance only if you have no hope for the future.

We left the keys with the neighbors.

A name that stands Alone.

The snow was melting in the garden and seeping into the ground.

In one day we edited twenty poems and went to a local restaurant in the evening.

Her husband wrote, "What days are these that I endure, and all because of your whims! Is it so difficult to write a few lines, or a letter every two or three days?"

There were small porcelain figurines arranged around the living room. Each one had a different pose, but none of them had faces.

Cape Cod: 8:45 in the morning. The conversation turned to the poem "Sold."

Their distinguishing features had been deliberately erased.

One of us was sitting in the kitchen, one on the living room armchair, one on the floor, and Tina had gone downtown.

Marriage is one of the primary reasons for the slow decay of individuality.

The woman checking my ticket looks drunk.

Everyone has to take off their shoes.

Including us.

Knowing just one language limits a person.

No one in this coffee shop has read Kurghinian.

It was March 16, and the next day one of us had to fly to Toronto, another to Los Angeles, and another to Bloomington.

And the city was hers.

If you're not married, walk confidently.

She wrote in her notebook: "Our husbands don't allow us to fall in love with 'strangers,' not realizing that oftentimes they are the strangers to us."

We must use the time given to us wisely and not waste it away in the marriage bed.

She also wrote: "One is dead if they don't have any hope for the future."

It's annoying to read with gloves on; it cuts off contact with the page.

In the near future they will erect big cities with tall glass buildings and people will speak many languages.

She says it's important to read simultaneously from four different books; goodbye.

2. COMING FROM OUR NATIVE LAND . . .

Here, there, over there—everywhere.

Yesterday Arkadii Dragomoshchenko wrote that sometime next week he was going to send the collection of unpublished essays.

Do you remember when Julietta Tomasovna kicked us out of class?

(*How Steel Was Tempered*)

"Why don't you say anything? I asked you a question, Avagyan!" And I . . . I am against reading such proletarian garbage—it's 1991, for heaven's sake, and you're teaching us according to the state plan.

(Two hundred years ago today they beheaded Olympe de Gouges in the streets of Paris for distributing pamphlets on "The Rights of Woman")—

this *one* is dedicated to you, dear Olympe. "Why are you silent? I asked you a question,"

Gohar Movsisyan also stood up. Naturally she would have tolerated one of us, but just then we became a collective—we were two against one. It was already a revolution.

We were both wearing brown uniforms, white aprons, and red scarves . . .

Do you think I've already become completely distracted from the book's original theme?

Listen: It's Miles Davis: *Live-Evil*, or the evil of evils; Keith Jarrett's on the piano; an awesome recording session: February 6 to December 19, 1970.

It's not important *who* it's addressed to, but *how*.

In his memoirs (see *Selected Works*, volume five) Avetik Isahakyan recounts: "She had an influential position among the young women, and they'd listen to her."

Don't you remember me? I always sat in the back of the auditorium by the window.

Arkadii, your essay dedicated to Margarita Meklina is quite deceptive. Some elements suggest that the excerpts and quotes are gathered and spliced together from an actual letter, but others contradict this reality and create an artistic illusion.

Today I wanted to send you a postcard, my dear, and for a long time I scrutinized the postcard stand

out of the hundreds of postcards I didn't find a single one with a suitable caption.

You won't be able to read it anyway since this language is foreign to you.

And besides, I don't have your address.

Steve Grossman: saxophone.

"There [at the Arghutian Girls' School] we became very close; I'd just returned from Europe, and she was about to graduate from the Russian Gymnasium of Alexandrapol. She said that she wrote, promised to show me some of her writing, but never did."

The days have become longer. Sometimes I hear the tapping of the spring rain outside.

Arkadii writes about a meeting on Nevsky Prospect.

I feel like we're getting closer.

Isahakyan was a young and lean nineteen-year-old wearing a black jacket and black shoes.

And she was eighteen.

In this picture she's third from the left, in the first row, sitting on the carpet with the dragon motif. Out of the twenty-four schoolgirls, she has the most mischievous look, as if complaining that she was forced to wear a uniform, and what's more, a white apron over it!

"The last time I saw her was at the end of 1907—in Rostov," Isahakyan continues.

No one is smiling; stone faces.

I'm going to try and translate it, but your style is very Steinian. I need to read your other books to grasp it better.

Send *Xenia*.

John McLachlan: guitar. Hermeto Pascoal: percussion and whistling.

Tired from the boring rules of the mud bath I finally left the sanitorium and headed towards the restaurant to eat dinner. However, seeing that my usual table was taken, I walked through the short tree-lined path and sat on a bench overlooking the lake.

In this notebook, there are five short stories all under the general title "Women."

My dear, sometimes I think that some kind of connection could have been formed between us.

One poet writes about another poet.

"She left the impression of an enigma: a true sibyl, a sorceress, an oracle—slender, tall, strong, with phosphorescent eyes—completely isolated from a family setting."

They were written around 1917–18, in the Kharkov and Yevpatoria sanitoriums.

And rather well rested, I wanted to get up when she sat next to me.

"A Meeting."

When you close the book and put it aside, you won't remember any of this.

Dave Holland: bass guitar.

In Isahakyan's words: "Though the idea of marriage or family were not for her, she was nevertheless a deeply loving mother. Yet, knowing that her calling was elsewhere, she suffered miserably from this tragedy."

I want to live, like the birds in spring.

The thick white hair was carefully combed; the [omitted text] quality of the combs bore witness to the fact that it had been difficult to heed the thrusts of time.

I look at her and imagine I'm pressing her grayed hair to my chest, while she seems oppressed by my observing gaze and tensely plays with her expensive rings.

Manuscript: II-5.

Today is May 1 and I want
to create this moment (not "take advantage of it")
to kiss, in gratitude,
the tired faces of the hospital nurses,
the guard in the neighboring watch factory,
the waitresses who run back and forth
in those ugly, cancerous coffee shops;
they've forgotten tenderness—
don't smile at them emptily; their stares are frozen

at your hand
that reaches into your breast pocket with slow conviction,
takes out your wallet and—

Arkadii offers a provisional title: "Dust."

"Perhaps you've lost something on my face?"

"I've only just found it," I answer stubbornly.

Chick Corea: piano.

I want to live, every day in another city.

"I remember vividly: she stood by the lamp, the light falling on her hair, uncombed and disheveled. She was reading from her poems with excitement. I was tense, completely moved by her pathos."

Khalil Balakrishna: sitar.

Herbie Hancock: electric piano.

Aram Ohanyan bought the photograph at the Vernissage.

Thank you, friend, for keeping it from the fire; although photographs don't burn, there's always the threat of humidity.

"When she finished, I approached her and kissed her hand," writes Isahakyan.

And here's my postcard to you, my dear.

True, it's not addressed, but what's important is that I'm sending it.

3. A DISTANT SORROW IN THE FLOWER-GARDEN OF MY SOUL

One day in the spring of 1926————————————————————

Lara, the book has two purposes: to recover what's been lost and to create something new.

Why is it composed of postcards? you ask.

————————————————————they were sitting in a café.

On which street, at which corner, figure it out for yourselves. Use your imagination. I'm not going to narrate everything.

But the city was Yerevan.

Of course the book has many purposes, but its main purpose is, *I want to send you a postcard, my dear, but I can't seem to find the right approach.*

She came with a walking stick. Her leg was in bad shape.

Zabel was jotting notes down in her notebook about the passersby.

A book you don't want to put down.

She takes off her white gloves and fixes her gaze on Zabel's pen.

SK: In 1898 Garegin Levonyan was the first from the Torgomyan family to utter a reproach, belittling me for holding a pen [omitted text], as the Russians say [omitted text] my writing.

To find the right words. To fill in the gaps.

But how do we uncover what's been lost without a trace?

SK: I will be the first Russian-Armenian woman poet.

Lara, don't you see this book's main purpose?

The difference between biography and autobiography is that the first one is finished and the second one is still being written; its course can change at any moment.

So it's plausible that the book's title could be "Auto/Biographies."

ZY: In Bolis they were also pushing me to teach—Armenian literature. But I had other plans.

The wind carries in the new scent of lilacs that mixes with the strong smell of dust after the rain.

SK: They talk to [omitted text] and they make confident statements about how I'm obviously not and will never be a poet.

But you ask: Who's the main hero? What's her name?

Where does the action take place?

Will there be an end to all this? A happy ending . . .

What's the book's title: "My Soul in Exile" or "To Live"?

Decide for yourselves.

With the exception of one manuscript, almost all of the remaining notebooks are dated.

My first poem, "At Night in the Valley," was published on August 23, 1898.

SK: I had other plans too.

ZY: But when they came and knocked on our door . . .

SK: At the end of that year, the railway gendarme L. told us that they were spying on me and that my name was on their arrest list . . .

ZY: . . . I wasn't at home.

SK: . . . we're going to Russia.

ZY: And a few weeks later I snuck into Bulgaria.

The sea, my dear, is very calm before the storm.

I'm watching the passersby and listening to Lara: "Her mother and son stayed in Bolis and her husband and daughter took refuge in Paris."

According to the science, blood and seawater share the exact same density.

Hurry on, my little boat! No smile or tenderness lasts for long in this accursed sea.

She had no other option: she could only write and tell about what had happened.

Write to live. Live to write.

It's *dark* my friend . . . and this endless path
                    Will never end;
I feel so tired . . . my sick soul
                    Weak and unfeeling . . .

Let me spread my book out beneath your buildings, let it touch your shins.

Let me write about love.

Disentangle yourself.

And disentangle me.

There is one purpose, which is to deviate from the original purpose.

I'll try and start again.

Lara, someone once said, one doesn't love again but loves anew.

To comprehend something new one must learn another language, customs, culture; in a word, they must live another way of life.

Outcast pilgrim, parentheses are like borders—cross them and you'll find . . .

SK: "Who are they?" I ask a Gogol look-alike. "The Russian proletariat," he says with a snicker. "They've called a strike to fight for eight-hour workdays, and for the managers of the factory to address them formally. Imagine that!"

Adorn me in yellow, orange, and bright red.

It's for you, but not only for you.

Nostalgia is more torturous in spring.

Reader, you are inscrutable, but you scrutinize me; you are dark, but you illuminate my nights; you are silent, but concerned for me; you know, but you don't confide; you are far away, yet touch my pages; you are familiar, but you reject me.

It's hard to get used to something new, but it's necessary to try.

SK: On May 1, I was carried away by the blue flood and a few days later . . .

Zabel examines her face intently.

ZY: A few days later I was witness to a horrible scene.

Setting a purpose is easy, it's accomplishing it that's difficult.

Close your eyes. Imagine one April day when the lilacs are blooming on the green bushes and the sparrows are sprightly again.

ZY: Bodies in damp ditches.

ZY: Mutilated bodies.

ZY: I, child of the East, had only seen suns there in the days of my childhood. Suns, red and blazing. Suns, whose rays reached deep inside me, penetrating my bones until they reached my heart

The book's title is "Reincarnation"—that's more appropriate.

Forgive me, reader.

And I'm someone who doesn't like making corrections.

Don't cross it out, just write over it with a pencil.

I'm drying a newly opened pomegranate flower on this page of the book.

A song for the night.

"My dear sister, let me kneel before your anguish,

Me, a constant captive of dissolute pleasure;

Let me take a bright spark from your hopes

And give light to my thoughts, abandoned in the night . . ."

It was here that I read her lines for the first time.

It was here that I understood the meaning of estranged heritage.

It was here that I cried helplessly.

Your eyes have grown dim; your pulse speaks
the languages of the Arctic Ocean, the coffin
holding your body shrouded with malice;
around you dance mournful beauties in black veils,
and braid your majestic hair with their dainty fingers;

and now, at this all-mighty hour, how can I not be afraid? How can I not doubt that my thousand-year-old cures have become old (from waiting) in their jars? How can I not tremble in excitement to feel the weight of your hands once more on my alienated skin—grown wild and scarred from the wrath of my own nails? Tell me, how can I? *My beautiful!*

Few understood our death, few remember our history, few have seen our resurrection.

Read Varoujan's "The Red Soil" now. Read Siamanto's "Vision of Death" today. Stand on the shores of the Euphrates and read Zartarian's "Nostalgias" in foreignness. Read them all on this moonless night.

4. HOW I WRITE AND HOW
I WOULD LIKE TO WRITE

It's useless, everything is useless.

One day in spring.

You smile at everyone except for me.

My grandmother would often buy tickets to the circus and take the three of us to see the show.

My throat would start tightening when the ponies, with their beautiful manes, would enter the ring.

The past never returns, but feelings, they do.

Re-cognized. Re-solved. Re-remembered.

They looked depressed.

First, the ponies would appear and run in a circle, one after another.

Then, a man in a black vest and a black, English-style top hat would come to the middle of the ring, whip in hand.

The crowd would begin to cheer.

He'd lift his right hand up over his hat and swiftly crack the whip over their backs.

The ponies were nearsighted.

Cast iron blinders were placed on both sides of their eyes, right and left, limiting their range of vision, so that they wouldn't get confused and would properly perform their tricks.

Drink this and take flight with Herculean might.

* *

Today I saw you on the fourth floor, in the English department of the university.

I'm going to read my wordwork "Letter to Violet" on May 5 in the Circus Room. Will you come?

At seven o'clock.

The Armenian version of the wordwork is included in one of the chapters of this book.

When I get up on the stage and start reading, I won't look at the faces of the people sitting in the audience so that I won't see you.

So that I won't know.

I'll just imagine you're sitting there among the spectators.

I'll just imagine my postcards are adorning your bookcase.

* *

My grandmother with her Chinese fan.

Reader, prepare yourself to jump through iron hoops.

The band rises to its feet; it's the triumphant moment.

Everyone's waiting impatiently.

We're going to jump through a ring of fire now.

Allez, hop!

That wasn't as hard as I thought.

Applause.

When it was over and we were all leaving the room, someone said that it would've been interesting to hear the Armenian version of the wordwork.

Somehow, you're lucky, reader.

Somehow, she was far.

Someone was standing next to her.

Tsvetaeva asks: Who is the "I" in the poem?

It's me, responds Mandelstam.

Tsvetaeva: What's the poet's story?

Mandelstam: This is it. Don't go looking for something else.

Tsvetaeva: How do I wait for TOMORROW?

Mandelstam: Renounce death and TOMORROW will come.

Tsvetaeva: How do I renounce death?

Mandelstam: By writing.

To study the stones, to learn from their demeanors, adopt their hardened expressions.

To be greedy with adjectives.

To describe the animate so that it becomes inanimate.

A short exercise: write a wordwork based on the element of repetition.

"Dogma."

Faith is a fox. The fox of all foxes.

Faith accepts the recognition of faith. The recognition of the fox.

Faith cannot exist alongside the fox. It's destructive. But. Faith is a fox.

This is the truth. Faith is a fox. The fox of all foxes. That's the way it is. Faith as faith must exist.

The fox nourishes faith. Faith is nourished by the fox. This is the truth. Because.

The fox is the truth. Faith is based upon truth. The truth is what it is. The truth is whatever you want it to be.

Faith says: I. Faith says: I know. Faith says: I know the truth. But.

The fox is what it is. This is the truth. Because. Being is a fox.

Faith is faith that reigns. Faith wants to reign over the fox. Over the fox of all foxes. But.

Of all the truths, the fox is the truest truth. Because the truth is a fox. The fox of all foxes.

That's the way it is. The fox has no faith. Because.

Violette says that exercises are useful and necessary.

The audience isn't clapping for the ponies; they're clapping for their trainer.

I've come up with a new title for the book:

"An Exercise."

To forget someone, and to remember others.

The portraits of Armenian writers from different centuries are arranged along one of the walls of the fourth or fifth floor of Yerevan Public Library.

Something's missing.

A lot of things are missing. For example, two sentences from this chapter are missing.

The most important part is missing, but you, my good reader, don't notice.

You don't ask questions.

For example, what would they have talked about if they'd met each other in 1926, one day in spring?

Or for example, why do some books never get published?

Or why is the National Academy of Sciences issuing its fifth edition of *Wounds of Armenia*?

5. SHE'S MY LAUREL AND THE MIGHTY MARBLE STATUE OF MY GLORY

I decided to take the long way home.

Bad wine always brings on a headache.

My dear, I'm writing yet another postcard. Writing without sending it . . .

I don't leave the house anymore, and I don't answer the phone.

Everything's become ugly and dull.

Yesterday I was reading Karslyan's new novel.

Not all attempts yield successful results; it's important to starve oneself as often as possible;

get lost in a foreign city and find the right way back to the hotel, that is, a temporary home.

I'm building a home out of postcards.

But every time the paper walls rise, a gentle May breeze blows in from the open window and knocks them down.

I'm starting again.

A book that doesn't have a title.

But that has perseverance.

This morning Lara wrote that tomorrow is the delivery day.

According to the doctor's calculations, the child will be born on May 3.

This time we decided not to choose a name prematurely so we don't find ourselves standing before an unprecedented reality.

Vayk was born on the fourth of the month.

And in the meantime, I'm sending you a few articles to be translated into English.

II-1, "On the Train," 1916, unpublished memoirs.

I was six years old when, after long deliberation, they decided to "provide me with an education."

They woke me up early in the morning and dressed me solemnly. They wet my hair and my father brushed it delicately, put it in a tight braid, and we went to church.

I prayed with the *Kirigan* in my hand, asking for "intelligence and grace, and to be obedient to my parents."

My father lit candles.

"Reverend Father, bless my daughter."

My mother and brothers followed my father and I outside and watched behind us for a long time; it seemed as if I were being separated from them and I wanted to run back home.

My father chided me, saying that it was already late, and accelerated his already quick steps.

"I'll escape later," I consoled myself, feeling the heavy weight of my father's palm on my hand.

We entered the convent, which was by the riverside.

My father was whispering about something with the short and stocky nun who kept looking in my direction.

"So, I get the meat, you get the bones," said the latter in a raised voice.

"No," my father answered immediately, his tender gaze turning back towards me. "Teach her only to read and pray; but my daughter is not to be hit or put to work."

I neared the doors as I backed up towards the wall. I looked outside and wanted to disappear when the second nun— younger, tall and pale—walked in.

"What's your name?" she asked with a kind smile.

I answered and began to cry.

Stolen heritage.

Saved from the darkness and humidity.

For you, reader.

Armenian-to-English translations are much easier than English-to-Armenian ones.

The Asmangulyan dictionary has been outdated for a while now; we need a new one.

Today I sent the manuscript to Diana Der-Hovanessian so she could get a sense of the poetry translations and write a blurb for the book's back cover.

Rowe's working on the introduction.

Or maybe she hasn't started yet.

These considerations were still underway between 1952–54 in the English Language Department of the Yerevan State Pedagogical University of Russian and Foreign Languages named after V. Bryusov, as they undertook the work of creating an English-Armenian dictionary that would contain thirty thousand words.

As this postcard is being written, the collection of forty poems is taking shape.

Her face will appear on the cover page, top right.

The phonetic transcription of homonymic words is given with the first word and is repeated only in the case when their pronunciation is different.

They say there's no demand nowadays for literary translators.

But several hundred years ago our scribes enthusiastically celebrated a holiday called the Feast of the Holy Translators.

The second Saturday of October.

She wrote that Micheline A. Marcom is still in Yerevan, and asked if I could send her the manuscript by next week.

I didn't think that Der-Hovanessian used email.

Somewhere it's already been said that one should "never assume."

In "A Word to God from the Depths of My Heart," Totovents writes, "Creator, there's no one who takes a staff, climbs the mountain, and speaks to you without a translator."

But again I've strayed from the main road.

It wasn't on purpose, believe it, my dear.

Governing thoughts isn't easy.

Still, as much as I restrain myself, her image appears in every object, and animates it.

The novel consists of postcards or telegrams that will never be sent to their destinations.

A question arises: So why write, and why postcards?

Usually, the postcard has two faces.

On one side there's a picture, something that embodies or symbolizes the spirit of its sender, and on the other side, a message.

The postcard is different (from other types of telegraphic communication) because it's "open" and every postal carrier can read it.

Thus, the contents of a postcard must either be neutral, consisting of empty generalities, or coded, encrypted in another language.

Aside from that, the postcard form itself limits the writer from excessiveness; that is, it filters her stream of thoughts, keeping only the crème.

So we repeat: the book consists of postcards.

Here they're at home, saved from exile.

Re-found.

6. THE INEVITABLE WILL CROWN US WITH AN INSEPARABLE CONNECTION

Every spring is perceived anew; this time from the perspective of a twenty-eight-year-old.

The inability to write is suffocating.

It doesn't matter who you're waiting for, but how; leaning back in a chair, cracking your knuckles as you go to the mirror every five minutes and in your head you repeat the first words you'll say to her when

> Who
> paces idly in there? Whose shadow is that?
> At whose
> gloom so enchanting has a lantern cast a light?

She was running after a shiny ball along the trails of a dark forest.

Trilingual words licked her wounds, lapping up the blood.

Playing with her skirt like the May breeze, lifting it up into the air, exposing her thighs and softly touching her lips.

Twenty-eight seconds in hell.

And released.

Second Interrogator: Where were you born?

Second Interrogator: What year?

First Interrogator: Why did you come back to your homeland?

Second Interrogator: Where were you living from 1915–16?

First Interrogator: What else did you teach besides literature?

First Interrogator: Did you assign your students the following books?

Second Interrogator: In 1917, on what grounds were you collecting money in Baku?

Second Interrogator: What were you doing in Iran?

Second Interrogator: Why did you go to Iraq?

First Interrogator: What do you write? Show us all your notebooks.

Second Interrogator: What was the original purpose of your visit to Egypt?

First Interrogator: How close were you to Vahan Totovents?

Second Interrogator: Under what name have you carried out your national activism?

First Interrogator: How many languages do you know?

Second Interrogator: Admit that you have led an anti-party life!

Second Interrogator: If you come forward and give us the names of the others, we'll let you go home.

Second Interrogator: Your husband, was he also a national activist?

Second Interrogator: Sign here that you agree to void all your writings.

First Interrogator: By the way, in one of the chapters of *The Gardens of Silihdar*, you brilliantly and uniquely describe your mother's nervous breakdown, or what the doctors call "postpartum depression."

Second Interrogator: I need names.

First Interrogator: But really, you depict her symptoms of depression so wonderfully.

First Interrogator: I'm simply enraptured. Allow me to kiss your hand.

Second Interrogator: Shut up when you're told to shut up and answer my questions now!

First Interrogator: It's all very interesting to me; I wonder if you've read Charlotte Perkins Gilman's book?

Second Interrogator: Don't pretend to play the hero. Here with me, everybody chirps like a sparrow sooner or later.

First Interrogator: And you know that the following sentence has been published in two different versions. I'm trying to remember exactly how it went;

"John laughs at me, of course, but one expects that _____."

The first version ends "in marriage" and the second "from a man."

In the beginning, the first version was published according to Gilman's preference, and then in the next edition, the second version. That is, it wasn't an editorial mistake.

Second Interrogator: Wipe up the blood. That's enough for today; we'll continue tomorrow.

First Interrogator: All this talk is probably boring you, please forgive me. Allow me to visit you tomorrow evening.

* *

Only delusional poets try to escape the constraints of form and content.

No redundancies:

Wordwork = prose − (a_x), (a_{x+1}), (a_{x+2}), . . ., (a_{x+k})

Elliptical quatrains.

Nothing motivates me to stay on this page with you.

Philip Glass and Ravi Shankar, *Passages*.

It's a recycled literary genre . . .

Until I'm released from this snake's skin and find a new one.

Sadhanipa: 8:31.

At the same time the poet must remain true to the beat of her heart.

The goal is not to confuse the reader but to implicate them.

For years you taught us how to distinguish poetry from prose.

But we still haven't learned that difference.

Prashanti: 13:37.

If I weren't forced to continue, perhaps this is where I'd end the chapter.

Tempo rubato | music | stolen time; an unintentional lengthening or shortening of the notes during a performance; a partial or temporary deviation from a strict rhythm.

She released the tourniquet and slowly the wordworks began to flow out.

Leave the best for last.

But how to decide what the best thing is?

Judging from her mood, she could have discussed someone else's literary legacy for hours as the Best Thing.

On the eve of the twentieth century, Sibil was the goddess of the literary salons in Bolis; she was the founder of the Patriotic Armenian Women's Association and director of teachers' training for women.

At the same time, Mariam Khatisyan was focusing on girls' education in Tiflis.

These different (bene)factories were producing the same old meek and docile angels.

But from their heights, how could these angels hear the voice of a fugitive woman sitting on the threshold of a church begging for a slice of bread?

"Sister, let me kneel before your pain," wrote Kurghinian.

She would steal warm socks from her husband's store and put them on the swollen feet of a street woman.

In the winter, when all the angels migrated to warm climes.

Now that I've finally seized your attention, it's time we separate.

P.S. Sometimes postscripts contain words of love.

P.P.S. However, they often end in clichés.

7. MY DEAR SISTER, ON THE OCCASION OF YOUR RETURN

Yerevan in the morning.

The streets are still wet from the nighttime ritual of the street sweeper cars.

Everything is closed, the people still asleep.

A true moment.

But that simple anointing ritual didn't exist yet in 1926.

Someone with a walking stick slowly roams through the city.

One of the authors of this book.

I know, you're still asleep, but I wanted to say "good morning" to you.

I called for another reason, of course, but just in case you want to know: the book has four authors.

At dawn, the sapling poplars are drenched in silver rays.

(How I wish I were next to you when you wake)

Sunlight pours through the curtains, flooding the rooms.

(to hold your sleep-drenched face in my palm)

Soon, the drilling of construction will be heard.

(to caress the happiness you deprive me of)

Stone-cutting machines will accompany the workers' baritone voices.

A New City is being built:

young women and men are working; their blue uniforms tightly hug their eager bodies.

In one of the streets, the kindergarteners follow their teacher, single file.

They are no one's and everyone's.

The schoolchildren roughhouse in the classrooms before the bell.

(but you don't answer when I call)

The metro cars rumble under the ground as they take the neatly dressed university students to the Yeritasardakan metro stop.

The foundations of the future buildings rise.

(you're not home when I knock on your door)

Under the directive of the head architect, the southern and eastern walls are being built with a new line of unbreakable glass.

(you send back my postcards)

The woman sitting in the café with an impatient face smokes her first cigarette of the day.

An open notebook sits on her table.

Someone with a walking stick slowly approaches her.

Two hands press together warmly.

I finally see the image of the New Woman, I see it and am delighted that I see it, and when seeing it, I don't feel anything but delight, I only see and am delighted.

Everywhere you turn, She's there,

wearing sturdy black shoes, her hair plainly combed, with bright, fiery eyes and a broad, powerful chest;

she's standing in front of the worker's station, in the library, on the half-constructed bridge, in the hospital, in the middle of the newly sowed field, in the university auditorium;

she creates the new; she is our Future.

The future is hers; the new is created by her.

Lara, it's not clear without an image of their faces. It'll be easier if we give names to the interrogators.

First Interrogator: Nshan Beshiktashlian.

Yes, people are going to need some time to think, and imagine while thinking.

It's impossible to remember everything, for example: the first-and-a-half postcard.

Or the faces of passersby on the sidewalk.

Or all the cities through which I've passed.

But it's impossible to forget Yerevan in the morning.

The catholicos-poet doesn't like your raven-black hair that juts out unevenly along the latitudes of the mid-southeast (you're too irregular and black).

The sadness of your eyes and impudent smirk are inaccessible to him—your difference, your distinctness . . .

Let's give the Second Interrogator the following name: Gostan Zarian.

It's important not to fall under anyone's influence.

But rather to walk alone, like Kipling's cat, along rocky and narrow roads.

Let's assume that it was about this "meeting."

Manuscript II-5.

I'd heard about her and had admired her from afar.

I look at her and imagine pressing her grayed head to my chest, while she seems oppressed by my observing gaze, and tensely plays with her expensive rings.

I look at her and want to read all the lines on her serious face; she turns toward me surprised; her charm not lost on me, she prattles gently:

"There are things from which a well-bred person refrains."

"I know that," I justify.

"Do you . . . ?" and her withered lips tremble like autumn leaves.

I look at her and want to know if she's lived much, if she's searched long, if she's lost something all too soon from the innermost depths of her soul, of her heart. I want to know what she got in return, what she's learned from life's lessons, and when she arrived.

She looks in surprise at my black, sunburnt face, and slowly a smile cracks from her lips.

"Perhaps you've lost something on my face?"

"I've only just found it," I answer stubbornly.

"You did . . . ?" She's already quietly turned her whole body towards me.

As usual, I pull her towards me [incomprehensible handwriting] her tiny hand into my wide palm and our conversation

* *

We agreed that I'd be their personal typist and editor.

Four authors and one typist/editor for all.

Second Interrogator: Your son has requested permission to visit you.

So be smart and answer my questions.

First Interrogator: The story's content is important only to give the reader direction.

A path to reach a certain idea.

Second Interrogator: Speak comprehensively—you're not in one of your lectures.

First Interrogator: Of course, there are different ways and paths to arrive at that idea.

Indeed, if we accept that the idea is definitive and within our reach.

Second Interrogator: What do you mean exactly by "national activist"?

First Interrogator: The traditional narrative form has its particular advantages.

It doesn't require any particular effort on the part of the reader or audience, just like Hollywood films.

Such a linear stream of thought serves only one purpose: to ease the process of perception.

However, if we accept that there are variable ideas, whose understanding requires more than just one uniform reading, then the text fades to the background, and unresolved questions come to the fore.

In a certain faraway city there's a street (I think it's called Arami) which rumbles when the metro cars pass underground.

Aside from just having a name, the street is lined by old trees and has a small, hidden pocket.

Big, old birches, whose lower branches are trimmed.

In the pocket are various works, fifty-nine of which bear her handwriting, including a piece with the title "A Meeting."

A meeting that will take place in an imaginary world.

Hanging from the hem of a tufa-yellow skirt, the pocket is quite deep; sometimes some writings get lost under the weight of others.

And when the roots of the trees, petrified from the movements of the metro, gently touch the pocket's lining, in the spring.

A thousand and one mornings.

Two hands press together warmly.

Forgive me—as I was walking, I deviated from the path; the new buildings distracted me; the city took on a whole new appearance; a whole new form.

8. BUT ONLY ONE BRIGHT RAY? . . . OH, THAT'S NOT ENOUGH, DEAR GENTLEMEN

When you read her book, it never crosses your mind how old and ragged or tattered her clothing was,

that there were no linens on her bed,

and instead of a pillow, notebooks,

as she lay in the hospital.

The head doctor was a short, bald man over forty.

Her leg was in an awful state, but she didn't want anyone to touch her.

She was alone.

Intolerant.

She tried to write with a pencil.

Despondently, she looked out the window, imagining the shore.

She wanted only two things: to listen to the murmur of the sea and to feel the burning rays of the sun over her naked body.

To get in the water and keep swimming without turning back.

The waves shimmer from the beaming of the sun.

"Hey, coy Eves of the sea, your language is not unknown to me, I'm not at all surprised how divers slumber away in your frigid arms . . ."

Her body is numb from exhaustion, and with every stroke weighs heavier.

No, someone's already written this;

Kate Chopin, I think.

Comparing the translation with the original, she said that the original hasn't been faithful to the translation.

To make it so that the translation is grander than the original.

Interview with the typist/writer/translator:

Question: How does one choose the right approach? How does one remain faithful to the text?

Answer: Gradually, step by step; in the beginning read the whole thing through, familiarize yourself with the writer's style, internalize their unique voice, see the world through their eyes.

Read their rough drafts, see and understand their mistakes.

Finish their unfinished sentences,

certain that your additions only balance or straddle their gaps.

Then read others.

Read them against the background of your author's text.

By comparison; reading the differences.

Then mentally translate

all your movements, comprehend all your words, which you exhale, invitingly, with a smile;

my task is to unriddle without betraying myself;

without forsaking unnecessary words.

But only to say what you want to hear.

My dear.

Nowadays in Europe they're trying to revive the epistolary novel, remarks the woman in the cinnamon-colored hat.

They're experimenting a great deal, and the majority of these works are based on Rousseau's famous text (*La nouvelle Héloïse*).

They're constructed around some type of obstacle. For example, the most prevailing motif is forbidden love.

The form of the letter enables one to create the illusion of reality,

as well as to satisfy the secret desire of reading someone else's words of love;

and, of course, to parody the old literary style.

Et cetera, et cetera, et cetera . . .

The European novel has enslaved all other genres;

the thing is that my country's literature doesn't interest anyone;

who reads Yesayan?

But I remember Tatiana's letter by heart.

Here, my dear, these are my lines to you.

Tell me, how does one find the right approach? How does one seize your attention?

How does one prove that this book is more than all the rest?

Endnotes:

While finishing this chapter it was decided to add another three to the forty already-translated poems.

While finishing this chapter everything suddenly became clear.

While finishing this chapter I wanted to say two things.

While finishing this chapter I received another email from Marc Nichanian.

While finishing this chapter she drank and took her wings.

While finishing this chapter we were trying to find celebratory words for a solemn closure.

While finishing this chapter an important meeting should have taken place but didn't.

While finishing this chapter something was lost.

While finishing this chapter one of the authors said: every day this book consumes me a little more, and every day it becomes more and more unbearable.

While finishing this chapter and before that.

While finishing this chapter and in this moment.

While finishing this chapter and after it.

While finishing this chapter, or never again.

9. THERE ARE UNKNOWN SONGS . . . SILENT AND VOICELESS

Second Interrogator: Your literary style doesn't correspond with socialist realism.

Second Interrogator: You disregard all of its rules.

Second Interrogator: You don't follow any of the methods of conventional style.

Second Interrogator: I glanced at one of your latest works and threw it away in disgust.

Second Interrogator: And you think that our people will read and be inspired by your "nationalist" or pro-bourgeois heroes?

Second Interrogator: They're not heroes, they're traitors and enemies! They all need to be burned, burned!

* *

Mediocrity.

Perhaps life truly is meaningless.

Perhaps her soul is in the darkest of places, and me: in a void.

No one can reach her, and she will surpass all of us and slip into incertitude.

"The Man."

Is sitting on a chair in the corner, waiting.

Hand in pocket.

There's a monstrous glint in his eyes;

fixed on the silhouette of the woman's body.

She's lying on the blankets of her cell bed with her clothes on.

Sleepless;

pretending to be asleep.

Every night her isolation ascends like smoke and hangs in the air.

From the corner she can hear the man's slow breathing.

There's something in his hand, but what, she doesn't know.

****

Second Interrogator: I must inform you that, from now on, we will keep your postcards in our office for the investigation.

Their contents are still incomprehensible to us and therefore —suspicious.

Whatever it is we don't understand, we condemn.

First Interrogator: Indeed, at the end of the nineteenth century, there was a concrete body of women's literature that had rich and unique qualities.

It was characterized by its parallelly constructed plots, the most widespread of which were the ones that included metaphorical representations of seclusion and escape.

In Brontë's book the elements of being imprisoned and silenced unfold on the third floor, or more precisely, in the attic.

The description of Bertha has a particular meaning. It differs from past descriptions of women:

her unrestrained, disquieting laughter,

powerful physical strength and size,

her thick black and uncombed hair,

the unbridled wrath that strikes everyone with terror, including her brother and husband.

The novel's meaning is hidden right in Bertha's image— she's present from the book's start to end and, I'd say, even beyond it. Her existence is reestablished in the works of the newer generation of writers.

She is the embodiment of Brontë the writer,

who directs and changes the development of all the heroes' lives;

the other heroes have secondary or tertiary roles;

they're necessary to keep the mystery of Bertha alive.

The book has three enigmatic endings; this is done in order to distract the reader.

Most literary critics hold on to the final ending, being as though they have no other option;

(the only option for them is to retire).

The first ending interrupts the twenty-fifth chapter when Bertha tears the wedding veil apart;

this is presented in the dream sequence.

The second ending: the main hero, a woman who's already received her inheritance, prepares to go on a journey.

And finally, the third: the main hero's wedding.

It's clear that Bertha-Brontë intentionally mocks the cliché of the English novel's "happy ending."

But let's return to our previous conversation.

It's important to remember here that not all books are published true to their originals.

Some things from the book are made to disappear.

Thus, while reading, one must be aware of the gaps where words were taken out to give them new meaning.

One of the authors suggested giving the book the following title:

"Mothers and Daughters."

Daring Girls who try to find their Daring Mothers.

It's easy to understand how certain styles or structures of life shape literary works that exist only in and of themselves.

However, it's much more difficult to comprehend how some (very few) works can become indispensable and live on for years and even centuries.

Second Interrogator: Tomorrow we're moving you to Leninakan.

Second Interrogator: No visits allowed.

Second Interrogator: We'll inform your daughter ourselves.

It's a lie, Sophie! Don't believe them. No one's going to inform you.

You must search on your own, you must find on your own, you must understand on your own, you must remember on your own, you must feel on your own, you must mourn on your own, you must be proud on your own, you must become on your own . . .

10. REVERSAL, OR PERIPETY

Today I woke up at six in the morning.

Creeping in from the open curtain, the sun's rays had strewn over this page in the book.

At eight o'clock, as usual, my neighbor's children slammed the door with a bang and went to school.

The root word *luc* or *lum* in Latin means (first)light: sun(rise).

After yesterday, my dear, it's difficult to concentrate on anything.

In one of the hunting scenes in Tolstoy's book————

When the postcards become fewer and farther between, you say I've forgotten.

But I'm completing your assignment with a schoolgirl's precision:

"I am writing about other things."

————————————————the greyhounds are chasing the fox.

And behind them a horserace of hunters; they wave their rifles in the air, egging on the dogs with their wild cries.

Two decently, yet modestly dressed women were seated in an open-air café on a Wednesday.

Woman with the cinnamon-colored hat:

"I've read some excerpts of your works; you write well. But what are you writing today? How are you recalibrating the words of yesterday that today have lost their meanings?

Woman with the walking stick:

"Some things vanish, slowly disappearing for a period of time, like with generations: the new generation rejects the ideas of the previous one, but the next generation discovers them anew, rethinks yesterday's words and structures tomorrow's discourse."

****

I've finally understood why I want to imagine their meeting in this book, one day in spring, on a day when it's both rainy and sunny and you're not sure whether raindrops or sunrays will fall onto your left cheek and fill you with some incomprehensible preconception.

When you love, you live without hope.

In this moment, and from this moment on.

You were smiling. Slowly sipping your wine, rose-colored, like your lips.

Only now do I understand why you wanted us to meet.

She was sitting next to you. Your hand resting in her palm. You'd think her palms were on fire, because my eyes were burning just there.

From this moment on I surrender my possessions to you— my everything—my only dowry and riddle; take out my eyes, take them out with the branches of an apple tree, put them on your sacrificial silver platter and let them dry . . .

****

Woman with the cinnamon-colored hat:

"There is a group that often meets in Stein's salon in Paris, how do I describe them—a group of eccentric intellectuals. Have you read any of her works?"

Woman with the walking stick:

"The name is familiar, but I haven't read anything by her. If there were more appreciation for translational work and a little bit more attention were paid to translation, the world wouldn't be this isolated. Yes, knowing only one language limits a person."

****

Woman with the cinnamon-colored hat:

"Her style is expressed through a certain language play based on the elements of memory. The word repetition renders new meanings, and the fragmented sentences disorient our learned habits of traditional reading."

Woman with the walking stick:

"Just like, for example, when you live in foreign milieus and in other circumstances, in different cities; a person's being doesn't change but is reinscribed with new meaning."

Woman with the cinnamon-colored hat:

"Yes, yes . . . words and phrases that are common and invisible to our eyes strike us in fragmented sentences because unnatural and estranged syntax slows the process of our perception and forces us to analyze each concept in a new way . . ."

Woman with the walking stick:

". . . and as time passes, everything becomes mechanically perceived (dulled), and the feeling loses its original (virginal) character."

Et cetera, et cetera, et cetera . . .

These thoughts can be considered either unique or imitative, depending on how passionate we are about writing theorems.

In reality, however, perhaps the woman with the walking stick would ask her interlocutor with the cinnamon-colored hat: Tell me, have you seen our orphaned children on foreign shores, have you caressed their heads with dark, thick hair, have you kissed their tearless eyes?

And she'd answer: Their tiny bodies, which recoiled from every move like beautiful snails in mourning, their raven-black heads with sheared-short hair, and their little black eyes, which out of terror had turned into unresponsive abysses . . .

＊＊＊

The Solitary Woman was written in Kharkov in 1914.

A play in four acts, which, however, still maintains the style of Greek tragedy: it's an *abab* rhyme scheme.

The first act opens with Heghine standing on the seashore, a white scarf over her shoulders, her right hand leaning on the boat's bow; she's lost in thought.

The captain, an old man with a "very pleasant face," says:

The sea is peaceful, your fear is in vain.
Would you like me to paddle along the shore?
Let's float up to the village.

This is a frequent scene in Kurghinian's works: a woman endlessly strives towards the depths of the sea, but something restrains her . . .

Heghine: I'm entering the sea for the first time / and I'm terrified.

In another piece, an early poem ("On the River Don," 1907), she writes:

... I'm scared ... this is the first time
    I'm on a boat;
I tremble from an unrecognizable fear
    I want to cry out.

Everything new inspires fear and it shows that people often don't wish to step away from their bedrooms (that is, their marriages) or even from their kitchens.

Why was the *Odyssey* considered an (extra)ordinary and heroic experience?

Because leaving any bedroom is already heroic.

And Heghine commands the captain: "Out to sea!"

* *

My Yerevan, the youngest, the saddest, the most beautiful of all Armenian capitals.

The hordes of foreign barbarians haven't passed through you, they haven't tainted your churches.

Your confidants betrayed you.

They abandoned you and threw you to the packs of dogs.

Tolstoy's fox has a beautiful coat and the hunters want to capture and skin it.

They think that they have the right.

Lara says: Let's go find her apartment.

"Our hearts pounding, we walked up to the Armenian feminist writer's house in Pera, armed with all the courage we could muster."

She says that she's found her last address from the letters she sent before her arrest.

"In the back of her spacious living room sat Srpouhi Dussap, dressed entirely in black."

Maybe they haven't destroyed that street yet; maybe the building's still there.

"We both seemed to have lost our ability to speak and had entirely forgotten what we had prepared to say."

In one of the most beautiful cities there's a street whose bosom is decorated with lilacs.

"Hearing that I hoped to become a writer, Madame Dussap tried to warn me. She said that, for women, the world of literature was full of many more thorns than laurels."

In the spring, the street erupts in white and purple fireworks.

"She told me that in our day and age, a woman who wanted to carve out a place for herself in society was still not tolerated."

There, reader—she lived in one of those apartments.

The garden of fountains, which most likely didn't exist in her lifetime, can be seen from the balcony of her apartment.

"To overcome all of these obstacles, I needed to exceed mediocrity."

She wrote these lines there, and later they became part of a novel that included autobiographical essays.

They might destroy this building soon, I say to Lara.

Perhaps the dogs still haven't been satiated.

After yesterday, my dear, I'm closing my eyes.

Don't surrender to my pleas, don't be elated by my words.

I'm preparing death's abyss for you, here, in the halls of my marble heart.

Leave, I'm warning you; I descend from the tribe of Semiramis's Arlez; don't come close, you'll burn your wings; I will devour you; I will destroy everything.

I'm building your mausoleum in this book; here, you will be immortalized.

April 25, 2005.

11. THAT'S HER, THEY SAY, THE POET

One of the chapters of the book has slippery features; we can place it anywhere we'd like and it will slide down, leaving three or four pages empty.

It doesn't belong to any part of the book.

It follows neither the previous nor the following chapters' contents.

A chapter that stands alone.

A chapter that doesn't have a fixed place.

A chapter that doesn't agree with any of the other chapters.

A self-contained chapter.

But the book is based on that slippery chapter; everything evolves from that letter to Violette.

Everything stems from an ideological interpretation.

Commissioned by the government, Hovhanness Ghazaryan writes the writer's biography in 1955.

"In December of 1903 she, along with her husband and children, set out for Moscow. However, the children fall very ill along the way so they get off in Rostov."

It's impossible to write the biography of a writer without referring to her work, because the writer lives through her book.

In other words, the pages of a book serve as an experimental space; here the writer produces thousands of drafts, creating countless scenes taken from various human experiences.

The writer lives through thousands of lives, and lives these lives not only in the present, but in yesterday's and tomorrow's lives as well.

"They initially settled in Temernik, and then later in one of the basement rooms in the workers' district."

"In that neighborhood she becomes acquainted with Masha, a worker in the Asmolov tobacco factory, who ends up looking after her troubled and impoverished family."

Ghazaryan was assigned to write about one thing only.

A Soviet literary critic's opinion had no right to deviate from the Original theme, but Ghazaryan was bold:

"Her deep feelings of gratitude and love for Masha is expressed in a rough draft of a poem she dedicated to her."

And he points out the draft book where one can find the poem, which begins with the following lines:

> We, as two separate planets, embraced
> each other on the threshold of a new life,
> I, a native child of the mountains,
> you, the Arctic's beautiful daughter.

Every type of difference was erased in socialist ideology, including the distinctive differences between the sexes.

So, all discussions around the differences of women's experiences were criticized and expurgated.

However, I think it's necessary to refer to the borderline consciousness of the poem, which is expressed in the last lines of the following verse:

> You stood there as a blonde brush
> I, a black and somber exile.

Here the dissimilarity between the two women is apparent.

Few Armenian writers have contemplated or examined the problems originating from discrimination, which materialize in the following manner:

Black = dark, filthy, demonic, foreign, ugly

Blonde = luminous, clean, angelic, acceptable, beautiful

All of this is embedded in the human unconscious, but, my little black darling, I don't have enough time to go deeper into this complicated issue, so I'll just mention the poem's last couplet:

We as two separate planets wept
equally under one great cross . . .

"The great cross" represents two vectors that intersect at one point, at a right angle.

However, the direction of the vectors can change at any given moment:

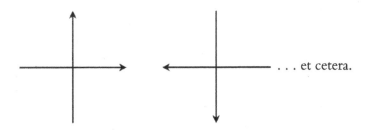 . . . et cetera.

This symbol surpasses the black-blonde dichotomy, stretching in different directions; the only thing that conditions the direction of its arms is the steel nail that unites and balances its trajectories; whichever way the wind blows, with its steel force, the nail will keep the vectors inseparable.

For her, there were no limits; she sought to find a common language for all, an all-same language—with different dialects.

Her only mistake was that she was alone.

That a real meeting didn't take place.

Instead, another meeting took place, around seventy years later.

Lara looks at my face and contemplates:

it's not always that we agree on something, and sometimes we even have arguments.

However we both know: the problem that we share is one and the same, and there are many ways to solve it.

Lara, we as two separate planets . . .

****

One of the authors suggested the first-and-a-half chapter should be inserted here.

The other swore, saying that that chapter needs to be omitted altogether; it betrays the book's internal structure.

The third silently smiled.

And the fourth, who was always the biggest proponent of experimental ideas, said that we literally "cross out" that chapter.

The typist/writer/translator intervenes here, pointing out that this type of experiment has already been done in literature and, by the way, with rather successful results.

And as a result, we again didn't reach any sort of agreement.

Dear Berj,

thank you for your caring work for guarding her letters and drafts all these years taking time away from your family to sit-and-wait in the reading hall through the cold winters in a hat

and coat waiting to meet and serve us graphomaniacs who
without sleep or rest return to you like lost children your
bright blue eyes that scrutinize my face your rough hands that
touch her manuscripts when you sweep away the accumulated
years of dust your tired voice that tells me of your lost youth
your dreams and disappointments your mighty Sphinx-like
posture that promises death to whoever answers your riddles
incorrectly I betrayed you my dear I betrayed your confidence I
became drunk from your care I quivered from your might I
gave in to the mania and yet there is a letter in this book from
which emanates inspiration vim and vigor and these pages are
embodied by her therefore excuse my temerity but see I am
returning it to you in a new casing preserved in a new cover
and envelope now it's your turn open up my riddle and leaf
through it find the answer . . .

12. A SHORT CHAPTER

Reader, know wisdom and instruction; remember the words of a genius.

In the autumn when we danced arm in arm around the grapevine in the fields of Shirak and

when the drums rumbled, resoundingly

when graceful brides circled around us with their handkerchiefs and

when broad-shouldered bridegrooms stood shoulder to shoulder to dance the dance of warriors and

when warm Areni wine flowed at the tables and

when the lavash flatbread ascended from the round, clay oven *tonirs* and

when the cool wind came down from the mountains and played with our skirts and

when the bards recited poems in celebration of the Day of the Holy Translators, words were worshiped and given heavenly power, taking flight with superhuman breath.

Superhuman, human, inhuman . . .

First Interrogator: It's been four days since you've touched anything.

First Interrogator: Hunger is not the way to struggle, you're wasting time in vain; I suggest writing—writing persistently.

First Interrogator: Let's make an arrangement; every day I'll come to you, you give me your day's writing, I'll hold on to it and then give it to Sophie.

First Interrogator: You can trust me.

First Interrogator: Write about all of this, write about our history, this country's bloody history.

Second Interrogator: This evening one of your friends ended his life.

In 1936, Totovents signed a contract with PetHrat (the state publishing house) to write a book of sixty printer's sheets in length about the idyllic past of the Armenian people.

The idea was Khanjian's, but from Totovents' heart.

Before that, he'd submitted "Apricot Tree," his new collection of short stories, to PetHrat; the book depicted the life of Western Armenians who'd resettled in Soviet Armenia.

While writing his book, he traveled through different villages, met with different people, and learned about their pasts and presents.

Totovents's novel was finished and was ready to be submitted in its complete version to PetHrat; however after the writer's arrest and apartment search, the novel disappeared.

"Apricot Tree" also went missing from PetHrat, without ever being published.

That year wasn't a good one, especially for manuscripts; they burned wonderfully, fast, and silently . . .

Out of the sixty-printer's-sheet novel only one short excerpt survived, from which they were able to get a rough idea about the massive book.

This autobiographical memoir begins with the hero's present and gradually expands into the past.

The conceptual goal of the work is hope, which acts as the naïve victim of deception, injustice, and insidious hypocrisy.

Totovents bitterly reflects upon the story of the deceived hope and faith of his generation.

Here, the genocide is presented in its entirety—the distant, (hyper)real past, and the tangible, cruel present—from the psychological perspective of the experience.

First Interrogator: The day before last they allowed a visit with his son. The whole time he was on his knees in front of his fourteen-year-old boy, his son's head to his chest, whispering something.

First Interrogator: When they came to take him, he tenderly kissed his son's lips and wiped his cheeks with his dry hands.

First Interrogator: In barely discernible handwriting, he'd written "Long live the Armenian people!" on the cell wall.

Nights have become unbearable.

I don't know what's worse, silence or the voices coming from the neighboring cells.

They came again today for an interrogation; they were in the next room for more than two hours, and five minutes hadn't passed from when they'd finally left and locked the door behind them that a muffled explosion filled the room.

I was awake, lying on my mattress, pretending to be asleep.

Five minutes and (then) despair . . .

What was he thinking about during those five minutes?

Then the sound of quick footsteps, they opened the door from the outside and entered.

13. THEY TOLD ME

The translated poems are being transformed; they no longer reflect the translator's handwriting but pass through guillotines of typographical corrections.

The first attempts at translation are pinned to her bedroom walls.

There are notes in pencil on each and every page.

Over the course of three years, the pages have yellowed and warped from humidity.

When a light spring breeze blows in from the open window, the pages rustle like silvery poplar leaves, fluttering and becoming alive again with the fresh air.

Dear Shushan,

Yesterday I reread her originals and your translations. Kurghinian is an old "acquaintance," and the material you sent refreshed my old impressions, which I didn't have the chance to express at that time (or perhaps I didn't have the maturity to express them). With this letter I'm going to try the best I can to offer an organized "opinion." My letter is in Armenian, and I hope you will be able to open and read it. I can see that the grace of translating hasn't been missed on you. So, I am leaving it up to your discretion to choose and translate into English whichever passage you find appropriate, and to publish it on the back cover of the book.

Shushanik Kurghinian is known in the diaspora mainly due to her 1947 publication. As far as I know, her 1981 publication received little response. But, as you see, the attempt to publish a selection of her works in a book was made only twenty years after her death. And it was a little more than a half a century after her death that serious literary critique and publication around her work began to form. A common trend, you might say. But it is so troubling when the matter refers to Kurghinian because she is one of the greatest writers from the eastern part of the Armenian world. It wasn't that she was or has been misunderstood throughout her life, after her death, and till now; it's even worse: it was a careful, intentional, and organized disavowal. First, in the form of tsarist censorship because of her socialist and revolutionary material, then by Soviet Armenian intellectuals because she was a rebel; and finally, by literary criticism (it couldn't understand her because she was a rebellious woman, that is, she was perceived by all as the most incomprehensible and unacceptable human type). A little later I will return to my use of "rebellious woman" or "woman rebel." I would like to focus a bit on the words "rebellious" and "rebellious woman," taking her example into consideration.

In the meantime, and referring back to the issues and conditions regarding the perception of her poems, I would like to say the following. First, the year 1947. A year of relative alleviation (due to which, [Gurgen] Mahari returns from exile, only to be exiled again a bit later). It is only because of this year of alleviation that Kurghinian's works are published. Yes, published, but what exactly? It's not surprising—they publish her most lyrical works, and let me say it again: at that time, the general impression about Kurghinian in the diaspora was that of a lyric poet who would write charming poems mainly devoted to love with a mildly revolutionary spirit— tastefully appropriate for those times. In the beginning of the fifties in Bolis, some of her verses were even used as the basis of songs. And I can assure you that the composers (consequently, the ones who loved her poems) were, to a great degree, people who were far removed (light-years away!) from any revolutionary idea. And *that* was the objective of the 1947 publication: to present Kurghinian as unthreatening; to neutralize everything in her poems that criticized social(ist) life and everything that was related to women's rebellion. Later in Armenia, the limelight around her was again misleading; again she was presented as the archetype of the Bolshevik Revolution (and, consequently, of the socialist status). What was the task of literary criticism then (and is it different nowadays?) if not to flatten its subject, adapting it to its political demands; to equate everything to its own *conventionality*, turning everything into something already familiar and clichéd? But Kurghinian wasn't easily digestible. Because she was a rebellious woman; a woman rebel. Her entire body of work was a rebellion; it was even more than rebellion; it was a challenge to the patriarchal social structure. That side of her work was completely hidden and denied by her readers, that is, by the people who found only love and sorrow in her writings; those who considered her to be a poetic precursor of the Soviet Revolution. The situation was the same in both Bolis and Armenia. How could they accept a rebellious woman, a woman rebel? They couldn't even conceive of the existence of such a person. It was unnatural for them. An unnaturalness, thus, rejected by rejection.

This is the reason why I find your undertaking so important, so necessary and so significant, when I see that women should have stood together to support their predecessor, translate her, and present her to the world. And it's not just a question of presenting. It's a question of saving—saving from backwardness, oblivion, and misrepresentation.

As I mentioned above, she was one of the greatest writers of the East. In any case, the first major woman writer. The only one who embodied rebellion. Do we know of anyone else who possesses her stylistic beauty, anger, perseverance (her continuous desire to write), and profound confidence towards her art? And of course she became a victim of rejection in her professional sphere. In the West, the only person who can be compared with Kurghinian in this sphere is Zabel Yesayan. Like Kurghinian, she was also married, adopted her husband's family name, and had children. She too, if not only to breathe, kept a geographical distance from her husband (she lived in Bolis while her husband lived in Paris). She is also part of a literary tradition that would be considered "feminist" today (but only in her articles, not her literary works). There are lots of similarities (especially since they were contemporaries) but there are many more differences. I would never consider Zabel a "woman rebel"—that aspect is not present in her works, or her life. And those same barriers of rejection, disavowal, misunderstanding, conventionality, and unnaturalness were not raised before Zabel. So, in this sense too, Kurghinian is exceptional. And I would want two things to happen: first, that somebody would publish the complete works of Shushanik Kurghinian (because as far as I understand even the 1981 publication is not complete, in fact, far from it); and second, that somebody would have the strength and capability to write her biography, this time putting aside the flowery words, the legends of the communist revolution, and emphasizing her instead as a woman rebel, the struggles, friendships between women and men, and the misfortune that comes as the result of all of these things. The time has come.

And now, as I mentioned, I would like to add some reflections that came to my mind while reading your translations. This time specifically regarding the words "rebel" and "woman rebel." The "rebel" would have never been accepted by the communists as the heir of the revolution, and in reality, not even before that. And not only from within the Soviet world. In 1952 the French writer Albert Camus wrote his beautiful book *The Rebel*, which caused such an uproar among intellectuals (it is currently forgotten and neglected but it played its historical role). And why? Because in reality it described that there had been a difference between the words "revolutionary" and "rebel" long before the 1917 revolution. The "revolutionary" was preparing the future Soviet regime and preaching inhumanity. The rebel was on the side of humanity. I am not sure, was that book ever translated into Armenian? Her rebellious stance alone was enough to keep Kurghinian on the sidelines of political movements. But the most unacceptable remains the "rebellious woman" (who is the embryo of humanity, the savior of humanity's honor). In those days, like now, a woman is supposed to be the base of the family, she is her children's mother, no? And when a woman rebels against the law which has befallen her, she deserves only contempt, scorn, enmity, or simply to be forgotten. She ruins the camaraderie. I mean, the phallic camaraderie of men. I have written on these issues once with reference to Violet Grigoryan's poetry (published in the journal *Karoun*). But when injustice and inequality—that is, the two extremes of social agony— are brought together (let's say, the general condition of being enslaved and the oppression of men's phallocentric system), the situation becomes explosive. Kurghinian bears another—a third—

extreme together with those two. She was not only a rebel (against the social hierarchy), or a rebellious woman (against the maleness of society), but also a writer who expressed rebellion in her writings (that is, made language her own, what impudence!). There have been very few people like her who possess all three qualities at once. This is what makes your undertaking more meaningful and necessary.

Marc Nichanian
Storrs, Connecticut
May 19, 2005

14. WE HAPPENED UPON EACH OTHER AGAIN IN A ROOM, ME AND THE SWEET-TONGUED POET OF THE WOOD

And so, my dear, I've finally gotten lost in your narrow side streets.

But before writing you the postcard I promised a few days ago, let me . . . respond to one of Nichanian's points.

In one of the previous pages I'd mentioned one of the paragraphs from *The Gardens of Silihdar*, the first sentence of which begins:

"We used to read Madame Dussap's books together, and in the work of that feminist author, we sought to find solutions to the problems we faced."

Kurghinian was also moved by those same questions.

Sitting in our tiny café, Lara and I are discussing those same questions.

Every spring brings with it new buds.

They blossom in the same old places, on the very same branches, on the very same sides.

Each and every bud is different from the other, however their features-(a)part are incomparable.

I'll try to put it another way.

We as two separate buds on one branch.

Each of our tree's buds has its own particular fragrance and place, and we need not compete with one another to absorb the sun's light and warmth.

It's not becoming of us.

One was a revolutionary, the other—a counter-revolutionary.

But together "we sought to find solutions to the problems we faced."

.dear my, aside everything put to want I, evening This

.you move questions these if as pretend Don't

.snake a like body your around coil to want I; black and thick, hair your braid I'll, fingers long my With

.time long a moment this for waited I've if even desires your to easily in give not will I

Delay = performative postponement

When my father wrote us letters from Ethiopia, I would tuck them away for a few weeks in the bookcase in our living room, right between Teryan's volumes.

My mother would get worried that there was no news from him.

And I was secretly delighted that I was in possession of the contents of those unopened letters, which I yearned to read with an uncontrollable desire.

But let the letters wait; let this expectation be prolonged.

And later, when I'd finally surrender the unopened letters to my mother—she didn't know the reason for the delay—she would get angry at the mail carrier for bringing them late, sometimes months later.

.dear, you to foreign is language This

II-1, "Conversations," 1907.

Dedicated to Miss K.A.: "Play a Bit More."

. . . and what do I want, I don't even know; I can't say. But keep playing, I want to listen . . . I want to be moved by your chords, I want to get drunk with the nectar of that enchanting sound.

Peaceful [omitted text], a love song, or solo, there's a yearning in the heart, it needs wings, it pleads for a kiss, a promise of love, a summoning of luck, to love love—to love each other . . . Let it go, leave . . . It's enough . . .

* *

You can read the book in different ways.

Some skim quickly over the words, racing through the pages.

When something's incomprehensible—for example, when the typist/writer cites another author—the reader refuses to "waste time" figuring out (clarifying) why the author's being referenced.

I'm not criticizing the laziness of the reader; I'm trying to rediscover their interest.

I'm trying to free and be freed

from the absurdities of *X Frames/Sec*

in the Introduction of which the writer says,

"We were trying to do it that badly that it came out well!"

When someone tells themself that the first literary experiment "came out well!," their literature teacher's job is to show them their first attempts at essay writing and compare them: Are they really that different?

Aside from that, Joyce is probably rolling in his grave.

In a word . . .

In the thirteenth century a brilliant man—who, motivated by his hunger for education, had earned the title of a monk in two different monasteries—was also known as a fabulist.

One of the monasteries where he lived for many years is today called Goshavank.

I'm necessarily considering inserting one of his wise riddles in this part of the book:

The fox beseeches the hare, "How is it that I am always hungry and you're always full?"

The hare replies, "Because I satisfy myself with whatever I find along the way."

I strayed again from my original path, my dear.

But I, like the fox, prowl hungrily; I can't simply be satisfied with descriptions.

Each postcard has its story; each word has its weight.

I weigh them with the stones of my heart.

15. TO THE SQUARE!

If this were the book's preface, I'd render the opening lines differently.

Perhaps like this:

Dear Reader, before continuing I warn you that many have irretrievably lost themselves among the pages of this small, poisonous book.

Or this way:

Friend, give me your hand.

With you, the turbulent sea is calm; for you, there is no path with me . . .

Second Interrogator: Sign right here: Hrant Dikran Yesayan. You only have half an hour.

A certificate of hereditary rights.

From 1937 on, Sophie writes that she'd become a Trotskyite.

. . . a veritable buffoonery of Soviet life . . .

Signed: April 14, 1940.

That was my brother's last visit.

Second Interrogator: We found a photograph in your apartment: you, together with Totovents; it was taken abroad.

Second Interrogator: You don't deny it . . . ?

Second Interrogator: Where was the picture taken?

First Interrogator: Last night I had a dream; let me tell you about it.

I woke up in the morning, and I went to the shower, carefully, so I wouldn't wake up my wife.

I turned on the cold water and stood under the refreshing stream; I stood like that for a few seconds; it was so pleasant.

A few random thoughts crossed my mind from yesterday's events, and then I reminded myself out loud not to forget to take a newspaper from the newsstand.

And then suddenly I heard a strange sound, something like wings beating.

I looked up, and there perched on the shower rod was a black bird.

It can't be, I said to myself and carried on as usual.

The raven-bird flew up into the air and began circling over my head.

I turned off the water in a hurry and wrapped myself in a towel.

"The time has come," I heard from above.

And you know how sometimes you see yourself from the side, like a director who controls all the actions and actors in a shoot? I saw myself just like that, on my knees, in the shower, naked.

I saw myself, helpless and frightened, and I couldn't intervene like directors do when something goes wrong.

Second Interrogator: Your son is very young, he's weak.

Second Interrogator: He was swearing that his mother was not a traitor of the nation.

Second Interrogator: On the contrary, he was insisting that you were a hero . . .

First Interrogator: But who does Virginia Woolf claim to be? What's important for her? What's most valuable?

Sitting in her room, she looks out the window: "Nobody cared a straw—and I do not blame them—for the future of fiction, the death of poetry, or the development by the average woman of a prose style completely expressive of her mind."

If opinions upon any of these matters had been chalked on the pavement, nobody would have stooped to read them, she says.

In half an hour, Woolf adds, the nonchalance of the hurrying feet would have rubbed them out . . .

But the national question matters to many.

Some people get so carried away with it that they begin to carve Mashtots's letters and cross-stones on the walls of their houses.

The Letters are valuable for Woolf not for decorating the walls of buildings but for reciting out loud and finding new meanings through recitation (or articulation).

To feel the presence of language.

To dis(un)cover phrases that have become commonplace and exa-*mine* their roots;

from whence have they come and why have they changed from their original meanings?

These letters, which we learn by heart—by h-ear-t—through memory and repetition . . .

Colorful people were walking along the streets of Yerevan; all of them to the square.

The city was familiar, but the people were unfamiliar.

One of the political activists was chanting energetically into the bullhorn.

"Everyone to the square!"

Two women lost in conversation were walking together in the parade;

towards Freedom Square.

16. AN UNBEARABLE CHAPTER

So we've reached the part where I abandon you, my dear.

You are my life and death;

I don't want to live without you, but life with you is unbearable.

But really, who was Virginia Woolf claiming to be? What concerned her above all else?

Why did she need a room of her own?

Why did she write her opinions when she knew that "the nonchalance of the hurrying feet would have rubbed them out in half an hour?"

A famous Russian literary critic would say that she wrote just to not let someone else take her place and bore us with their absurdities.

This book is composed of a thousand and one inner monologues;

the monologues of different people.

For the typist/writer/translator this is the most acceptable literary mechanism since she has to grapple with writing down the thoughts of four different individuals.

Thus, the book can have a title like this:

"A Collection of Unpublished Monologues."

In his letter Marc Nichanian points out a vital premise: the poet's consistency, her unremitting desire, her urgency, her need to write.

One of the poems begins like this:

"I've disowned, forgotten you, truly . . ."

It was written one year before her husband's death.

In 1917 Arshak Kurghinian was vacationing with his children at their family summerhouse.

In Rostov.

One evening they were sitting among friends in the shade of the balcony.

Drunk on wine, Arshak decides to swim in the river.

He'd bought the summerhouse for his wife, being that for years she'd dreamt of living on the water's (the Don's) banks.

In one of her poems, exactly nine years before this infelicitous event, his wife writes, "Hey, coy sea-Eves / I understand your language; / I'm not surprised that in your frigid arms, swimmers shut their eyes."

The group of friends, with their exhorting cries, watch the lonely man's passage.

A passage without return.

Some could describe that moment as "weakness."

In that moment the man realizes that it is impossible to quell his desire, and desire drowns him.

His wife, whom he had loved, whom he loved, to whom he wanted to give everything he had, wasn't his.

She had never and would never belong to him.

That is, they were married according to the rites of the Church, but nothing was as simple as that in real life.

But let's return to our previous discussion.

Nichanian knows that this ingenious woman couldn't have simply lived with proletarian sentiments;

she was paving the road for her future daughters.

In the post-revolutionary years when Armenia had already become a member of the Soviet Union, when the workers of the world had already united and overcome their strife, Kurghinian persistently continued her criticisms regarding women's issues;

here's a passage from "The Refugee Family":

A fervent fury of dread and tremor
Grows deep inside my heart
The woman, whom I left in serfdom, asleep
Has not yet seen the day's light . . .
And has fallen into a deep sleep . . .

The poem was written on January 14, 1922—

during one of those brutal winters, when another Shushanik fell victim to starvation;

Vosdanig Manoog Adoian's mother.

In despondent moments, life sometimes appears abstracted.

* *

The poems can't offer to my despondent and yearning soul what my heart desires. They are only spiritually comforting . . .

I know that living with me doesn't give you any satisfaction; well, you'd need to live someplace; live in my home, but in your heart and in your soul live for anyone and anything you want . . . I haven't existed for you for a long time now.

My life's inception began all wrong, and wrong it will deteriorate.

I—a man of life. You—fantasy's, nature's, and beauty's minstrel. What complete opposites we've been . . . What to do? It's destiny . . .

It's unbearable for Anoush, the poor girl! What days these are that I suffer . . . Is it that hard to write a few words, a letter every two or three days? There's no end to my anger . . .

The letters were written from Rostov.

Sent to: Anapa.

It's late already, let's go.

We leave the museum and cross the street; there's a little café there.

You know, Lara, a translation, like algebra, requires one to find the precise formula of the relative values; the sole formula.

For example: there is x word or phrase in the sentence to which you must give a value or explanation so that the translating sentence can balance the translated sentence.

The simplest thing is also the most bizarre thing, and the most bizarre thing is also the most wonderful thing, which has to be examined.

That most simple x word is the key to the sentence that will open that foreign door to that foreign room where, locked away, they keep the foreign books about foreign cultures written by the hands of foreign geniuses.

It will show that somewhere in the farthest and most remote part of the world there's also someone who's afraid to lose the sensation of life.

That she is also looking for the meaning of life every day, every second.

Knowing that when the voice that was dictating Tolstoy's Arzamasian terror and the Maid of Orléans's vision appears again, she will have to obey.

Kneel before the raven-bird . . .

The task of the typist/writer/translator is to show humanity that life evolves at a spiraling pace.

They say "farewell" when they know they'll meet again.

When they utter it at the moment of departure, it seems like people are separating for a long time, perhaps forever.

But life evolves at a spiraling pace, it spins back and forth, in curves and circles, every time in a different direction, and it always deviates from its path.

So, farewell, my own—

17. NO NEW ARMENIAN WRITER HAS INSPIRED ME

She was afraid to live a life that was the same as everyone else's.

She was different from the others because she saw the future differently.

The future began with divorce.

Just like this book.

Her poems were being translated over a very long period of time.

And "a long period of time" means four years.

Forty poems—in four years.

She knew that it's impossible to love just one thing in a lifetime.

Or one person.

It's intolerable for human nature.

Simply unnatural.

Let's pose a banal question: Who's your favorite writer? Which is the best book ever written?

One of the answers could be: it depends on your mood and how the day went, or on the artist's ability to captivate me with their art, giving new life to the things I already know but in a way that seems completely new, virginal, not yet made conscious . . .

The typist/writer/translator finally understood this when, throughout those four years, almost every day she'd find a new meaning in the poems.

At one point, in her opinion "Demon or Angel" was the most powerful expression of existential philosophy.

Indeed . . .

Who had dared to murder God in this way, "holding that titanic captive under my heel"?

Zarathustra, you might say.

But it was not murder, nor was it nihilist conspiracy; having rid herself of Aeschylus's myths, like a Fury—spirit of revenge —she had come to occupy her rightful place.

She emerges "flames ablaze," diabolic and powerful.

Like a bolt of lightning, just one of her electric glances could illuminate an entire city.

The poem was written on May 20, 1907.

But it was printed for the first time in 1981 in the fifteenth volume of Mirzabekyan's *Literary Heritage*.

Then came "The Waves."

In one of her notebooks there's a short essay in which two women are talking:

The woman interests me like the new paper delivered in the morning—a new word, new page, new news—everything is due to the great [incomprehensible handwriting], thanks to which we live, and which we hope to revive.

Reader, here is yet another unpublished excerpt from that same notebook:

However it's incredibly frustrating to me that men are considered "above" us; are considered powerful; why are you smiling?—here's an example for you: When I got married, my husband was a lion; he'd enter the house triumphant, exacting, obstinate. This lasted several years; he was my perfect master, and I was so captivated by him that I had completely lost myself; the purpose of my life was to please him. And one day I rebelled . . . let's switch places, I resolved . . . a storm raged on in the house, but I didn't give up. I took the reins of my house and husband into my own hands and it's been three years now that I've been unfalteringly moving forward. Now I too have needs and desires . . .

And now, reader, let's return to "The Waves."

> The waves—were accustomed to the black cliff,
> the waves—curled under the shorn cliff,
>> always coy in their cadence,
>> rippling from the gusts of wind,
>> fondly greeted the cliff
>> with a bustle of an active life.
> The waves—rebelled one black day,
> the waves—sang an alarming song—

If you want, reader, I can easily point out the wave-cliff/woman-man metaphor and interpret it.

But is it really necessary? And besides, I don't want to make everything ironic.

I'll just reference a few lines from "The Fisherman," which was written in 1908.

> A wave is a woman; every woman, a wave;
> Love, a boat without rudder or oar
> To the knavish heart, but a trifling play-thing,
> That after the storm will become a corpse . . .

After which the translator's attention is drawn to the poem "Again."

Three quatrains. The first of the translated works:

"See the autumn sun turn pallid," that which gave color to everything, and everything was illuminated by it.

At night when it gets dark, I start looking for you, my dear, in this strange city, at the tavern, I wait—hidden behind the trees.

My terrible sorrow . . .

I search for you everywhere, down every street, under everyone's arm, in everyone's embrace.

"Unnamed, my sorrow writhes within," and I greedily search for a new ideal, a new interest, new ideas . . .

When the sun fades, a myriad of other suns shine in the sky.

"Like a demon, I want to love again—like a demon-preserving . . ."

Again doesn't mean that it is or isn't possible to forget the past.

Memory preserves everything and when something new comes along, new experiences and feelings stand side-by-side with the old ones and refresh them.

Past phenomena are repeated, but we perceive them anew.

Another poem that was written in 1907 is now read with new eyes; different images come to mind, however we all know what it's about:

"I pity you, dull-witted women, / for chasing after rouge and beauty aids, / wasting away your time without a goal."

A few students from the Department of Management at the Yerevan State University of Economics cross my mind.

Or the couples sitting in the café at Hotel Europe . . .

"For having a subtle instinct for marketing, / selling yourselves for the highest price, / bickering endlessly over style, appearance, / a circus show of fashion rivalry."

Et cetera, et cetera, et cetera . . .

But how to write the history of this new generation, asks Zabel?

How to represent the future when they are trying to erase our past?

You propose we destroy everything and start again; is that even possible?

Is it possible to do away with a living civilization, an entire culture, and insist that it didn't exist?

To murder a new mother and teach the child a foreign language, a foreign religion?

To build a future based on lies? Tell me, is that kind of life possible . . . ?

—It appears that yes, it is possible, unfortunately, in any case, however, it doesn't matter, yet, but, nevertheless, it's still the responsibility of each person to find their own truth.

To have a principle, an initial source from which the heart's first beat emanates.

The greatest sin for each faith, each language or culture, for each person, is forgetfulness.

To forget the truth.

To forget the fox who has unblemished fur, quick feet, and eyes umber like the desert.

To forget the hunters, who from dusk to dawn wait hidden behind the bushes, rifles cocked, knives sharpened, to possess that beautiful and immaculate animal, to seize its pelt and smother the spark in its eyes.

18. THERE WAS NO WATER
IN THE DESERT I CROSSED

Most unbearable is the night when they order all lights out.

My dear daughter, I'm writing an autobiographical novel, the continuation of my first book.

It begins in 1915.

The rough draft of the book is almost ready, and I think the working title will be "Comedic Exile."

One of the guards promised me that he'd (secretly) pass it to you.

Try to publish it in Paris, at Comrade Krikoriantz's publishing house.

* *

Out of the darkness, the silhouette of a faintly visible train slowly, clankingly approaches the station and, letting out steam, comes to a halt.

The conductor, dressed in soldier's garb, opens the door and one by one ushers the people lined up in the station onto the train.

A woman in black clothes and a hat, holding a small traveler's bag, enters the train car and settles near the window.

She takes the daily paper out of her bag and immerses herself in reading.

****

Out of the darkness, the silhouette of a faintly visible train slowly, clankingly approaches the station and, letting out steam, comes to a halt.

The conductor, dressed in a blue uniform, opens the door and one by one ushers the people lined up in the station into the train.

A woman in black pants and a necktie, holding a suitcase in her hand, enters one of the cars and sits in an empty seat.

From the pocket of her suitcase she takes out a stack of photocopies and starts to carefully examine its contents.

II-1: "On the Train," 1916.

An unpublished autobiographical essay.

I feel guilty when I think back on Nichanian's words.

I'm guilty because for four continuous years I haven't been able to think about anything else.

It's as if this train were moving out of time and space.

And for that reason it's impossible to measure the speed of its progress.

****

The endless steppe sprawls outside the window.

It makes no difference that each time I sit in the train car I'm filled with a new feeling of anticipation . . . at the same time my soul gravitates towards familiar sights.

Suddenly, without warning, one can easily lose sight of their life and purpose in this vast steppe.

Here, one might not seek but find her untimely end.

* *

Out of the darkness, the silhouette of a faintly visible train slowly and heavily slithers through the desert.

One of the train cars carries political prisoners.

The one sitting by the window is writing: my heart gets tight with a strange and incomprehensible feeling.

It's impossible to explain this passage, this train car filled with strangers passing along the edge of the world of obscurity.

Hour after hour the train stops and the conductor herds new groups of people aboard.

Their silent faces are riddled with the same expression of infinite despair.

It seems we've already resigned to our fate.

It seems that the country has entered "a sad era" and it seems that I am embodying it.

* *

You can find any word you wish in a dictionary, but brilliant writers write in different languages simultaneously.

Or, as W. Benjamin would say, they're searching for a pure language that embodies all languages.

Her book begins in Scutari, in the neighborhood called the Gardens of Silihdar.

However, the writer doesn't present it as someone who's seen deportation, persecutions, death, powerlessness, or disappointment; that is, as someone who's seen life.

But rather as a child who's seeing and feeling for the first time.

That is, with new eyes.

To see and assess things on one's own terms.

And what gives the book that uniqueness is the writer's masterful rendition of precise and unexpectedly raw details.

In this way, for example, she presents the story of a father and daughter, a relationship in a world all their own, the sustenance and beauty of which is revealed in the following line:

"The steamboat rocked from side to side as it passed through the Marmara. My father and I were sitting and talking on one of the benches along the side of the deck . . ."

The book is unfinished, or more precisely, finishes with that trip.

Where is this train of thought taking me?

I don't know, but nevertheless the train continues its march; that journey that began in the green gardens of Silihdar and passed through the literary salons of Constantinople, Cairo's orphanages, Paris's universities, the brilliant minds of Yerevan, and Stalin's concentration camps, all the time heading towards the steppes of eternity.

19. AT DAWN

We've got to free ourselves of the Anna Karenina syndrome.

Indeed, some just aren't cut out for entering into marital relations.

Some don't feel obligated to "breed a nation," especially when they know that the world is already overpopulated.

Yet, for centuries humanity has frequented the "marriage market" and today it seems to have an even more attractive aspect.

Different kinds of markets exist.

The village, city, internet, international, et cetera.

And each one of them has its own laws and rites.

But let's not stray from our theme.

But before turning to the main theme it should be parenthetically mentioned how the work of the translator can easily turn into something clownish.

They give the translator typist/writer the black-and-white costume of a mime and thrust her onto the stage.

Her face is covered with greasepaint, and a tear is marked on her left cheek like the Harlequin.

She is forced to recite her own translated poems, which don't contain a single phrase of (her own) inspiration.

After the editorial analysis and emendations the manuscript retains neither the poet's style nor her triumphant voice.

And the translator stands like that upon the stage; her mouth moves but the words don't come out.

Aravot luso . . . "Morning light," sings the church choir.

In February of 1896 Arshak Kurghinian writes, "Lilia *jan*, my dear, I'm suffering from doubt because you don't understand me. What to write . . . ? It's enough . . ."

The letter is addressed to a young woman in her twenties who was preparing to leave for Moscow to continue her education.

In reality, however, her name had appeared on an anti-tsarist list.

That is: either escape, or be exiled, or both—what's the difference?

"It's been four years since we've encountered many incidents and obstacles while together. Why did I leave Tiflis and end up here [Alexandrapol]? Do you at least respect me? Write! Console me!"

"In my eyes, everything's lost its old charm . . . friends, relatives, parents—they can't console me. I don't have anyone to encourage me and dispel my sorrows in your absence."

By the way, this is not a biography.

Each and every work is based on a true story.

And even if it is utterly unacceptable in a literary work to insert a footnote to indicate from where the quoted lines were taken, one of the authors considers it important to inform— perhaps the reader would like to go to the museum archive and find the aforementioned letter and read its entire contents, being that, out of four pages, only a few lines are quoted in this book—anyway, one of the authors thinks that it wouldn't be excessive to mention that the above mentioned lines are from letter IV-3.

Sometimes it's possible and also necessary to break free from certain canons.

V. Rowe's blue-jacketed book is an important and progressive volume among biographical works.

Aside from the biography it also includes textual analysis.

The last two chapters of the book are especially interesting: "Socialism and Revolution: The Poems of Shushanik Kurghinian" and "Exile and Genocide: Zabel Yesayan."

It seems that the writers were considered in separate chapters, isolated, but what unites them is the era and Rowe makes that entirely clear.

The book was written in English and published in London.

And for as much as it seems strange to read Armenian women's history in English, it seems even stranger that Armenian women are ignorant of and disinterested in their own history.

And really, what's the need in studying a history whose entire existence, every second, is a struggle?

And how does one study a history that, every time it tries to plant its roots, is uprooted?

But this history is old, reader.

Old, unique, and complex.

At dawn. I'm waiting for dawn.

When from the sun's first glance, my room will catch the unrestrained fire of awakening.

I wish you, reader, dreamless nights; when, in your sleeplessness, you will contemplate yourself, try to find yourself, and understand what it is you want from this life.

20. RAQUELLESSNESS, OR DON'T FEED ME DREAMS

There's the following description in her unpublished autobiography:

"Our family worshiped two things blindly: the music played on the *tar* or *saz*—the *bayati*s of the passionate East—Hafiz, Shiraz, Sayat-Nova, and Jivani, and the other was the Bible, Gregory of Narek, and the Psalms which were read grandiloquently, drawn into ecstasy by the hashish of religious poetry . . ."

And under her bed she secretly kept books, among which were Gogol's works, Chekhov's stories, and Tolstoy's novels.

At night when her brothers would fall asleep, her mother would often see the flickering candlelight from their small room, come inside and scold her.

A ten- or eleven-year-old girl with big and examining eyes.

When I was ten/eleven years old, my father would often take me to Khnko Aper Library. I am trying to remember the face of my first librarian . . . it was long ago . . . she would help me choose books, chat with my father, and ask us to return the books on time.

I was never overdue with the books.

Every day my father spent one hour on my reading; after dinner we would sit together in the living room and he would make me write down every new word and copy its definition from the dictionary in my exercise book.

But a hundred years ago that same girl with big and examining eyes wasn't allowed to read.

Actually, it wasn't that she was not allowed, they simply had different plans for her.

* *

In 1904 she started to write a play in Rostov, which was taking place in a Russian town, the heroines of which were seamstresses and factory workers.

Of course, there are also the owners of the factory and their delicate, graceful wives, but they take second stage.

Anton loves Martha.

But Martha rejects Anton's hand, refusing to become his assistant and follower: "Would you have preferred I lied and fooled you and became an obedient wife and created peace in the family, a peace disguised in deceit and outrage . . . ? No, I can't. I am not attracted to personal pleasures; there is no peace for my turbulent soul. Don't stand in front of me . . . let me go . . ."

In order to save her mother from poverty and starvation, Martha starts to sell her body—since the salary from the factory was not enough, and they were drowning in debt.

But the mother, who in the play symbolizes everything that is bound to the past, dies.

In the last act Anton meets Martha again in another town.

Martha has turned a new leaf; she's a Red Cross nurse now.

Anton (*longingly*): Where are you going, what are you going to do? Oh, Martha, how is it possible to look at life so triflingly?

Martha (*bravely*): I am *going to the people* . . . I will go, I will work as much as I can, and I will always write to you about me . . .

Anton: And then . . . ?

Martha: And then I'll come. (*Longingly*) You won't forget me till then, will you . . . ?

But Arshak couldn't forget her; he waited till the very end.

He wrote letters without any hope that she'd answer them. Sometimes he'd receive postcards from different cities.

He was faithfully waiting for his Martha's return.

The play is called *Red Cross*.

* *

It's important for the writer to see the beating heart, hold it in her hands like a wounded bird fluttering wildly, feel its rhythm, and then describe it to you, reader.

A book which is necessary to finish but impossible to end.

Every book has an ending, but this book differs from the others; it has neither a title nor an ending . . .

On Sunday, my dear, I thought that everything was over between us . . .

Raquel-less-ness

I was talking about meaningless things, driving on unfamiliar highways; it was the last day of spring and . . . Raquellessness.

One hopeless Monday—drowned in waves of desperation.

"It's over," I was saying.

But at two in the morning I was woken up by the ringing of a telephone.

It was a dream.

Or something like a dream.

It was her; she had left a message . . . I've got to erase it from the memory.

Martha asks, "Anton, what would you like from this life?"

Anton answers, "To be with you forever."

Martha continues: And I would like to be understood; historians always distort reality, impoverish our history with lies, but in order to understand that, it's necessary to devote yourself to life, understand its inner structure, see it from all sides through everyone's eyes and to share your own with them.

Sometimes, reader, the typist/writer forgets to put quotation marks around cited words or sentences.

Does that mean she steals others' words?

Which is worse: To let the living words of the poet die in damp boxes in dark, treacherous rooms or to sow them like seeds, mixed with another's words, to revive them and let them bloom in untitled fields?

Besides, quotation marks privatize words and make them someone else's property.

The words belong neither to the typist/writer nor to you, reader.

They simply unite our past, present, and future.

21. TAKE AWAY MY LONGING FOR OUR NATIVE LAND

The national radio is broadcasting one of her poems.

Have you ever heard how Vera Hakobyan reads poems? You can't find anybody like her in our city today.

Lara says, "Me—in an Armenian ghetto; You—in Soviet Armenia."

And then adds, "We as sisters separated by fate."

In 1922–23, just like seventy years later, different citizens from different parts of the world desert their surrogate homes and return back to the Country.

A country where somebody can lose her freedom or life.

A fate that decides to play a trick one April day.

But the blue moss that grows on the walls and dome of the ruined church——————————————————————————cannot grow on someone else's walls.

Their roots penetrate deep into the crevices of the tufa stone.

It was at the end of 1922 when Vahan Totovents left the "luminous darkness" of the West and came back to his fatherland, to settle once and for all, determined to live and work here.

Inspired by bright visions of the future . . .

What does it mean, to (re)claim?

Lara replies: When from your childhood you read about a country where the people speak in old and familiar dialects, where the pomegranate juice is thicker than blood, where the mountains change their color and mood under the sun, when you hear your grandmother's nostalgic song—that infectious love hidden in the deep wrinkles of her black eyes; that loss which will never be recovered; those familiar, strange people, who smile openheartedly and freely; that familiar, strange city, which you discover every day; that familiar, strange septuple fountain, from which, drinking, you can at last quench your thirst; those familiar, strange streets which lead you to the square; the familiar, strange monument that's called Mother Armenia.

A few minutes later she adds: There was another one in the place of that monument, do you remember . . . ?

Yes, without you, my sister, the country was drying up; the fatal years of drought followed one after another.

In those years a son was obliged to renounce his father, refuse to have any relationship with him.

A daughter was forced to betray her own mother.

Not for thirty rubles though, but in order to save other members of the family—her brother.

Sacrifice one in order to save the others . . .

Many were confused in those years.

They lived without hope and loved their country.

It all seems incomprehensible, even "absurd," to the contemporary writer because they are young and haven't lost anything yet in life.

They can't understand how, in the morning hours when Hakobyan's voice would resound, her diction and rhythm would spread through the city like an electric pulse . . .

And they write about certain Bakzals.

And imagine that they're creating postmodern works.

And deny that they are simply copied from someone else.

But copying is not a bad thing in principle; in fact, it's even necessary for novice artists.

It's necessary to know the great geniuses and understand their instruction.

In classical Armenian the word "instruction" had several meanings, one of which was "truth."

I'm forced to repeat: Bakzal cannot find anything in his reflection in the mirror because it embodies the absence of authenticity.

Or the instruction of others.

Et cetera, et cetera, et cetera . . .

One of the authors of the book asks when we are supposed to finish this project.

They're waiting for me outside; it's late, let's go.

****

One day in spring.

But it's not often that time in the novel coincides with real time.

"Real time" had progressed quite a bit, and what was left from that spring day was just one important letter.

And though Arkadii Dragomoshchenko mentions how he feels the slow flow of the day from the calendar in one of his essays (I simply imagine a cheap, page-a-day calendar hanging on his kitchen wall, with information on the health benefits of herbs on the flipside of the pages), it seems I am still standing on that cozy street, underneath which every six minutes the metro roars by, and I feel the soft spring zephyr on my face.

I think it was Tuesday, around two o'clock.

I was standing on the opposite side of the museum and smoking my last Akhtamar.

From out of nowhere a twenty- or twenty-one-year-old boy appears in a leather jacket, holding a huge bouquet of flowers in his hand.

He introduces himself and very politely offers the bouquet.

I refuse.

Not because I don't know him or feel uncomfortable.

Simply, what would I do, enter the museum with flowers?

He insists persistently, saying he wouldn't go away until I accept the bouquet, and I persistently refuse.

The sky was dark, just as it would be in that square, on that day, at that time.

They are waiting for me inside, it's late . . .

And suddenly, when I was walking through the corridor of the museum, I noticed the bouquet in my hand.

And Berj was sitting in the reading room.

22. ON BLACK NIGHTS WHEN THERE ARE NO STARS

Her parents also came back to the homeland in the late 1920s.

The Committee of the City Soviet had decided to settle them in a village and give them some land.

Berj's grandmother and grandfather were Armenian literature teachers in Van.

But, how does one write about real events, which in reality have become fairytales?

How does one write it, but not as a history text?

Here the reader might think that the book doesn't have any sort of structure or direction.

That it's impossible to write a book with no heroes.

That in the end it's necessary to give the book a concrete title.

That the author is simply tangled in her own thoughts and doesn't know how to find her way out of the very story she's begun.

The reader is mistaken.

The book has four—or five?—authors who are as different as the seasons of the year.

* *

Almost every day at the same time Berj places the brown bundles on the table, where the number of the archive and its table of contents are carefully written.

Each bundle is like a hydro station; the deafening pace of the water floods the turbines and spins the iron wheels.

My dear, when I touch the rough paper of the bundle, it seems like I'm touching your estranged body.

Erik Truffaz Quartet: *The Walk of the Giant Turtle.*

Cool. Frozen: My bones can't get warm . . .

Belle de Nuit: 6:08.

Every week is like a century.

Turiddu: 4:25.

Every meeting is like the last.

Seven Skies: 6:46.

Frightened fingers, numb with desire and awe.

The book is based on a scandal.

To be more precise, it's based on one unpleasant incident that took place in a museum, when an original letter disappeared due to the carelessness of one employee.

It would be fairer to say that because of one employee's boundless trust, a manuscript copy, in which the most important formulas on human relationships were hidden, was lost.

The letter began in the following way:

"I want to write that I love you, but I don't know how to write it so that it comes out right."

23. I'LL WANDER AND ENDURE . . .

By socialism, Lara, it didn't cross her mind that those democratic, sublime ideas could turn into such false concepts.

It made her just sick to see how senselessly unequal the national wealth was distributed and how pointlessly and without appreciation it was wasted.

". . . And my heart wept, seeing compassion trampled in this world,

Where desire for possession is the never-ending goal."

When human life was turning into a tool of exploitation for bloodthirsty aims.

She was talking from the depths of centuries.

Yes, she was against the church and Christian faith; not against the Christian humanist ideology, but rather the phenomenon of how faith had been turned into a tool to make people senseless and defenseless, and to enslave them.

She wanted it such that each and every individual could decide and find their own truth in life.

She wanted to have the possibility to seek and find.

A country whose inhabitants would care about their surroundings, a community whose members would understand that their existence and success depended on each other; on their united strength.

United strength, where diverse and myriads of lives have the right to exist.

If she knew how the Soviet critics would exploit her poems, she would have rather made a huge bonfire in her apartment to burn them all, then gathered all the "sold" (girls) so that they at least could warm their frozen, bloodless bodies.

In Rostov, Kurghinian would often bring home girls who sold their bodies at the market.

They were (her daughter) Anoush's age, fourteen or fifteen years old, pale, poverty-stricken girls who, in their life's moment of desperation, didn't have anybody to take care of them and help them get back on their feet.

In the poem "The Flower Seller" she writes:

In truth, why is she a bad girl,
or has nothing, knows nothing at all?
Why has no one embraced her with love,
why is she starving, why battered so?

This particular issue really got to her: society's judgment of the "fallen" and their behavior as a moral issue, insisting that "natural" womanly virtues gave way to obscenity.

How society flaunted a falsely pious lifestyle.

How boundaries didn't exist for men and that the selling of their bodies was considered virility but for women it was an abyss of shame and death.

He that is without sin among you, she said, let him cast the first stone on the "fallen."

She'd often take warm socks and fresh bread from her husband's store and go to the market.

With old and tattered clothes
With beautiful eyes of azure,
She is the child of great anguish.

[. . .]

To the crowded market full of people
She comes pale, lifeless, and hungry
Looking for an "acquaintance."

This poem is called "The Girl," but in her drafts Kurghinian had titled it "The Fallen One."

More precisely, the first title was "The Girl" and then Kurghinian crossed it out with a red pencil and wrote "The Fallen One" over it.

When this poem was published for the first time in 1947 in the *Collected Works* compiled by Mkrtchyan, the editors chose the first title: "The Girl."

But it wasn't mentioned anywhere in the footnotes that the work also has another title, which is essential and gives the work a deeper meaning.

Anyway, this book doesn't try to criticize others and their omissions, and neither does it want to color the memory of one simple and bright woman with lavish words of praise.

This book embodies an epoch.

Or more precisely a day in spring, when two huge icebergs were about to merge in the depths of the literary ocean.

Their collision would provoke a series of disastrous quakes below the water.

That brute force would create a new world, or even worlds: in one of them, Lara and I are sitting in a little café, talking to each other, our eyes filling with warm tears.

Let's get out of here Lara, it's late . . .

24. AND THEY SWUNG FROM THE INFAMOUS GALLOWS OF THE DARK PRISONS

After long years of wandering, being lost in foreign cities, crossing through the deserts where the sands still whisper with the murmurs of blood, I came here, I came to find a new life, I came to be revived.

I've come home.

An unconventional home, where the windows are very low and so I kneel each time in order to look out from them, knowing that whatever I see is worth my kneeling; there, on the other side of the window bars, stretches my city with its feverish ghosts.

Repel your rays, brilliant and luscious, take off your clothes —white, beaming; wear the pale!

It's strange . . . I thought I had found you.

Now from the window I see how they are destroying your old two-storied houses—with wooden balconies and tiny, narrow yards—and instead building identical high-rises and apartments where identical people live.

The wounds never heal—they become postcards; postcards that are written and sent to unknown addresses, and melt in the hands of unfamiliar readers.

****

You write to me: Come back.

In celebration of your return . . .

But Lara, Yesayan wrote letters in two different modes: first she wrote to keep her work going, that is, she wrote for them (the interrogators); then she wrote for herself, that is, she wrote whatever she was really thinking.

So let this book be my return, my coming back home.

This road is difficult and unstable.

Very often I deviate and become obsessed with other ideas, which seem to be irrelevant, but without these deviations and mistakes it's impossible to realize and assess the threads that weave life's dragon-carpet.

Thus, after long consideration, the Second Interrogator who also thought himself a poet, had come to a very important conclusion, which was that the less other writers wrote, the more attention and praise his own books would get.

The man of such glorious ideas would of course sometimes even tremble from excitement as he would begin to imagine how he'd be crowned best writer, and he'd never lose the chance to derogate and preach to other writers about their tendency to lay claim to xenophilic ideas.

Only this way and no other way, he'd think.

Because when interrogators ask questions they already know the answer.

The only and correct answer that they want to hear from your lips, your torn and bloody lips, bruised from the blows of rough hands . . .

If only I knew how to stay faithful to you, my dear.

Again you return, you are always on my mind.

But my love turns to poison, and as soon as you approach I slowly, flirtingly clasp your delicate neck, hanging long and tongue-tied, kiss you; kiss you with my cold lips, and when you look at me you get lost in the dark depths of my eyes, as if hypnotized, and I kiss and kiss you and then gently sink my fanged teeth into your neck . . . oh my pain . . . oh my love

* *

When the Second Interrogator lived in Paris, they called him "Little Russian" (maybe because he was short).

Datevik Hovanesian: *Come and Lend Me Your Ear.*

The Sky Is Cloudy: 4:20.

The "Little Russian" loved a woman much older than him who, in turn, loved a German who was in prison for murder.

The Breeze: 4:11.

In literature, new ideas emerge mainly when old and familiar concepts are (trans)ferried from one form to another.

When they pass from one hand to another.

For example, recently I met a silversmith at the Vernissage who was selling earrings that were crafted with some unique details.

They were old buttons that were made in the previous century in an atelier in Zangezur.

But the earrings were very beautiful and considered a novelty.

In this way ideas travel from century to century—transforming, wearing new clothes, fashioning new hairstyles.

For the things which the Second Interrogator condemned others, the "Little Russian" pursued (xenophilia) in a heartbeat.

Come and Lend Me Your Ear: 6:31.

For his beloved woman he was ready to "spread golden suns before her feet, declare war, bomb the Bastille and free all the prisoners, including her beloved German."

The Brides of Mogue: 4:14.

And over the course of his entire life he wasn't able to express his love in his mother tongue.

I Am Burning: 5:52.

He didn't understand the Armenian woman.

Rather, he did not search, did not find, and when he finally did understand, it was already too late.

They'd already transferred her to another prison, from where they sent everyone by train to Siberia.

Without return . . .

25. SOME BLACKGUARDS . . .
PROUDLY PINNED DOWN . . .
MY INVINCIBLE WING

Reader, you can't imagine how much I was taken by one of her poems called "Return."

Each time when my mind travels back to Yerevan.

Some things change their appearance, however, the same old men are always sitting in the park with poplar trees; they are serious chess masters, though they never participate in international tournaments.

Many kings and pawns have passed in their lifetimes; they know how a queen can disarm a whole army in one move.

But more importantly, they know that every game ends in defeat, and starts again with the expectation of victory.

This book doesn't contain any novel ideas.

It simply (re)visits the main events of the past, and tries to understand the present, which is incomprehensible.

Yet the brilliant writers (who never did meet each other) were writing about their realities with such clarity and foresight that even after a hundred years their ideas have remained so relevant.

. . . And when each time my mind wanders back to Yerevan.

The new streets being built over the byways are losing their habit of deviating in the city.

You can't find the truth, Lara, unless you deviate.

This city was theirs.

They were both walking through the labyrinthine byways, talking as they deviated from the main road.

They were talking about what characterizes a person's anti-heroism.

How to understand the prerequisites of the title "hero"?

Is the antihero she who abandons her husband and children, an affluent life, and a comfortable house in order to be close to the people who are deprived and raped by society?

Or is the antihero she who has no gravestone and will always wear the "traitor of the nation" crown of thorns upon her forehead?

Or is the antihero she who dares to criticize the Writers' Union as well as the literary critics who ignore and distort our history?

Anyway, reader, know that this book arrives to you incomplete.

In the lines you see the (*) mark, know that in these parts the most potent words from the original text have been removed.

Every book, especially a collection of translated poems, goes through a "cleansing" process.

For you, reader, because apparently the editors know (and know well) what you need, in what quantity and in what form.

. . . And when each time my mind wanders back to Yerevan.

I finally understand everything.

How, my dear, I got lost in the coldness of your eyes.

Marietta Shahinyan has a series of interesting works, her first impressions and memories of Soviet Armenia being of particular interest.

But here I'd like to recall one poem (she wrote very little in this genre):

I know that when wounded
the clever animal crawls into its nest,
so then heal my pain, native land,
the pain caused by the northerner.

The poem entitled "To Armenia" was written in Russia, where Shahinyan was born and lived most of her life before her return to the homeland.

From 1927–29 she rented a room in the workers' district of Dzorages and started to write a novel about the construction of a hydroelectric station.

* *

The beginning of the twentieth century is marked by visions of utopia in the realm of urban development.

In the context of private land ownership, the value of the urban land (especially in the center) was so high that the land owner would never agree to grow trees instead of a profitable building.

For this reason, a city covered in green was only a dream.

In 1918 Alexander Tamanian escaped to Anapa, unable to bear the situation in Petersburg caused by the revolution.

Many intellectuals had found shelter here.

Just like M. Shahinyan, who'd given a section of her apartment to the Tamanian family.

He heard about the first Republic of Armenia from Shahinyan.

In fact, he began drafting the general plan during the years of the first Armenian republic, and then he continued to work in Tabriz after he was forced to leave Armenia because of the Bolshevik Revolution in 1920.

In one of his reports addressed to the Soviet government after returning from Tabriz he wrote: "The improvement and development of Armenian cities await their turn . . . on the basis of the western European city-garden model."

In 1924 Tamanian presented the general plan of Yerevan to the Council of People's Commissars.

Or in Charents's words, "a sunlit city."

. . . And when each time my mind wanders back to Yerevan, I want to get lost in its luminous passageways, rustle with its trees, remember the past, feel the present, and see the future . . .

This book, reader, is doomed.

To be more precise, we can think of it as an imaginary Space, where there are real elements, or in the words of a certain Frenchman, we find ourselves in our self-created heterotopia.

26. CONCLUSION, OR "RETURN" TO THE BEGINNING

A book of postcards.

A book that, throughout its creation, changes and distances itself from its original aim.

Because it (perhaps) embodies an unknown cemetery . . .

My postcards have stopped, but because of the impossibility of our relationship, my dear, the book is almost ready.

Whatever's impossible to solve in reality, I'm trying at least to understand by writing.

There is no stranger feeling than the betrayal of a loved one.

There is no greater pain than the first drops of disappointment that poison your veins.

When (at the cost of death) you accept that blow, that lethal slap, at that same moment comes freedom of the soul, an infinite freedom.

And perhaps, sitting in the train, she was writing about that, about how tears welled up in Hrant's bright eyes, and with what strength he suppressed them.

Through her coldness she was giving strength to her child.

Some kind of instinct prompted her to think that, no matter what, she must not inspire hope.

Firmly holding the pen, she was writing how her boy's kiss was still burning in her left palm, where a hidden, unsuppressed tear was trapped by chance.

Those lines that she was writing, that book which was to become her entire life's story, consisted of more than truth; there were things there that we'll never find in the papers or encyclopedias.

When she was still a student at the Sorbonne, little Sophie would fall asleep under the lamplight.

While she, sitting in the corner of the room, would write.

The room was cramped and there were books scattered everywhere—on the floor, on the table, on the windowsill.

A response had arrived from the *Dzaghig* monthly asking her to write an essay entitled "The New Woman."

By morning the essay is ready and she, leaning against the window pane, lights a match and, with tired fingers, brings it to the cigarette between her lips.

The warmth of that match also burns my fingers.

Here, sitting on the translator's uncomfortable chair, many months after that spring day.

I am holding the manuscript of forty poems in my hand.

The flame's yellow tongues greedily consume those excessive, ugly expressions that the anonymous external editors had added/changed.

If you don't know what it's about, then I beg you please don't distort the essence and meaning of the work!

Don't make it "comprehensible"!

Reader, perhaps these lines are also directed at you.

* *

In 1917 Shushanik Kurghinian writes a poem that you might say was dedicated to Zabel Yesayan.

I say "perhaps" because in reality that meeting never took place.

The poem begins with the following lines:

> She's become old from looking at the chains
> And has forgotten gentle manners;
> Tattered hair, clothes unkempt . . .

Many didn't know what life was like in the Russian tundra. Many people adapted and lived without asking questions.

> Her mature demands were seeking ways out
> And stormed the heart of the noble girl
> That the free mind doesn't have fortune in her country
> And she was swept into the arms of the vortex. . .

Here she is talking about Bright Ideals.

When the body turns into a heterotopia.

When it becomes necessary to get rid of family bonds; when neither mother, child, nor husband can understand the inner aspirations and pursuits of your soul.

When the thought of "happiness" becomes relative or completely loses its meaning.

When physical pleasures slowly lose their importance.

When the only purpose to live becomes to rediscover not the story that didn't exist but the one that was deliberately made to disappear.

* *

The life shortened by years in Siberia
Brings sad and dark images to the mind's eye . . .
Impudent mockery, insult, beating, and hunger—
How many, how many innocent victims they've reaped . . .

[. . .]

But the longing for the inglorious homeland
Takes the alert mind far into the heights
And burns a sacred flame under the chests,
Against which, both prison and death seem feckless, so
feckless . . .

I'm looking fearfully at her face,
My sister, in celebration of your return, come stay with me—
Let me pray for you, let me beg for your life,
Since it was for our sake that you forgot about yourself . . .

****

Here, reader, there need be no words.

TRANSLATOR'S AFTERWORD

DEVIATIONS

Memory (the deliberate act of remembering) is a form of willed creation. It is not an effort to find out the way it really was—that is research. The point is to dwell on the way it appeared and why it appeared in that particular way.

—Toni Morrison,
*The Source of Self-Regard:
Selected Essays, Speeches, and Meditations*

*When the only aim to live becomes to rediscover
not the story that didn't exist but the one that
was deliberately made to disappear.*

—Shushan Avagyan, *A Book, Untitled*

"I beg you, please don't distort the essence and meaning of the work! / Don't make it 'comprehensible'!" What is a translator to do with such a text that beseeches against its own distortion, while at the same time declares that among its many goals, its "one [primary] purpose . . . is to *deviate* from the original purpose"? When the translator aims to do justice and relay the source text to a reader while also preserving the inevitable strangeness of a

text in translation, at least one thing becomes clear: *Dear reader, you are not reading* Girq-anvernagir. *You are reading* A Book, Untitled. *If you want to read* Girq, *learn Armenian!*

One day in autumn.

I first encountered *Girq-anvernagir* [*A Book, Untitled*] in a season of my own deviations. I was considering throwing in the towel on the graduate degree I'd started at Ca' Foscari University in Venice, Italy. Months prior, I had been schooled by my mentor, a gentleman of the collar, that there were no Armenian women writers of real literary merit.

What did exist, perhaps with the exception of a mediocre few whom he didn't even bother to mention by name, were of little import and certainly not worthy pursuits of serious intellectual critique. He was visibly agitated that feminism was to blame for destroying the image of the Armenian matriarch. But anyway, he said, there was little sense in bothering to read these unnamed women writers when there was no greater literature in the Armenian canon than the neo-Romantic poet Misak Medzarents, or the lover of neologisms, Daniel Varoujan. It was either my callous unfeeling or naïve misappreciation that couldn't sympathize with the sad fate of the young and dreamy Bedros Tourian—poor one, who'd died of tuberculosis before his time, and with a love unrequited!

I supposed that *no Armenian writer inspired me*. With my aesthetic critique clearly off or my nostalgic longings just not up to snuff (did it matter which?), I left Venice, unsure of any return.

Till one day in autumn, *when each time I wander back to Yerevan*, I anxiously sat on a concrete porch that opened onto the unkempt backyard of the ground-floor apartment two of my friends were renting, and where I was couched, on yet another in very a long line of hospitable couches that nomadic year. My friends had set up a home office in the living room to help edit a book they'd worked on with an art collective. Later that evening, the rest of the *équipe* was going to join. That book, *Queered: What's to Be Done with Xcentric Art?*, was to become material for the next one, *Zarubyani kanayq* [The Women of Zarubyan].

The arrival of these women—one an artist/photographer, one an artist/graphic designer, and the other a literary scholar/writer/translator—made me more anxious than excited. What was I to say for myself? That I'd dropped out of my program, that I needed to abandon my career in literary criticism and find a new path? I remember sitting out on the porch, the trellised grapevines overhead starting to chill in the autumn air, the bugs circling the lightbulb, the cast-iron chairs that held our cheap Areni wine (the days before the fine wine boom in Armenia) and velvety cognac, and as they left for the evening, her saying to me, *So Deanna jan—dear Deanna—go back and finish what it is you need to write.* She was about to leave Yerevan—a self-imposed exile—and return to Normal, Illinois, to get back to her translation of Viktor Shklovsky's *Bowstring: On the Dissimilarity of the Similar.* I wasn't sure then if misery wanted company, or if she'd noticed my spark rekindle over our discussion of (with the exception of a notable few) the limits of literary criticism in the Armenian world and how we imagined it differently, but before she left, and after the kind of hug that implied a potential, future kinship—inviting, but with trepidation as to not over-inscribe—she wrote a modest note in a book with a red-and-white cover. She handed it to me silently as she walked down the steps. "To dear Deanna—with warmest wishes, Shushan." And so began a journey, renewed.[1]

Girq-anvernagir was published as samizdat in 2006 in Yerevan, the capital of the Republic of Armenia. Yet the book itself—initially written as a translator's diary while Avagyan was translating the poems of Armenian writer Shushanik Kurghinian into English—is the product of a series of exiles, longings, and returns over the course of a century. Forging a home for herself in the United States by writing in her native tongue of (Eastern) Armenian while on an indefinite sojourn, Avagyan's first novel brings together the stories of four women from the "eastern" and "western" contexts of the twentieth-century Armenian reality; women separated by a hundred years as well as by the shifting borders of the empires and nation-states that necessitated their constant migrations. In Avagyan's rendering, *one day in spring*, they all meet in Yerevan.

The first encounter in the novel is between Shushanik Kurghinian—the socialist poet who fled the Tsar's regime to return to a Soviet Armenian republic—and the Western Armenian, Constantinople-born writer Zabel Yesayan—who had fled her own annihilation as the Ottoman Empire fell and the borders of the modern Turkish Republic were drawn. Kurghinian's works were censored by the Tsar's regime and disingenuously represented and derided by Armenian nationalists; in post-Soviet Armenia, her work was forgotten. Yesayan, whose influential works were largely overshadowed by her male contemporaries in the Armenian literary imagination till the early 2000s (and not in small part due to the great interest sparked by the archival labors recounted in this book), fled ethnoreligious cleansing in Ottoman Turkey, and was killed later in Soviet Armenia by Stalin's regime. Yet in 1926, the year in which Avagyan sets their meeting, the lives of both women overlap in Yerevan: Yesayan has just arrived in the Soviet Armenian capital, and Kurghinian dies there one year later, in 1927.

However, Avagyan's staging of this fictional encounter between Kurghinian and Yesayan is precipitated by an equally important one in the novel's present. Again, *one day in spring*, three quarters of a century later in Yerevan—the capital of the now-independent Armenian Republic—the narrator (ostensibly Avagyan), referred to in the novel as the "typist/writer/translator," meets Lara. Avagyan—who is translating Kurghinian's poems—had already left the post-Soviet Armenian republic in the early 2000s for the United States. On a visit back to her home city of Yerevan she begins to work with Lara Aharonian, a contemporary whose family was deported by the Ottoman Empire and who thus grew up in the Armenian diaspora—first in Lebanon and then in Canada. In the time the novel is set, Lara is a recent migrant to Armenia who comes to research Yesayan, and when she and Avagyan meet, they decide to join forces and search through the state archives together to look for traces of these nearly forgotten authors. Later, Avagyan would publish her translations of Kurghinian's poetry in the United States as *I Want to Live: Poems of Shushanik Kurghinian* (2006) and Aharonian, along with Talin Suciyan, would direct and produce the documentary *Finding Zabel Yesayan* (2008) in Armenia and Turkey, marking the first significant wave of reinterest in Yesayan's works.[2]

In many ways, then, the lives of these four women are parallel. Just like Kurghinian and Yesayan, Avagyan and Aharonian were separated by political borders and cultural contexts and thus, speak two different variants of Armenian—Eastern and Western. And just like Kurghinian and Yesayan, the two contemporary women's political subjectivities and migrations are conscribed by the modern inheritors of the empires and colonial states that continue to wield power and write the dominant narratives that define their respective geopolitical contexts (namely Turkey, Russia, the United Kingdom, the European Union, and as the dominant global power, the United States). Though Avagyan's and Aharonian's migrations may be read in one light as a choice of circumstance, rather than a flight for their immediate and physical wellbeing, it is questionable whether we might interpret their movements as privileged choices rather than as matters of symbolic, social, and cultural survival in their own right. In the first instance, one must consider, after the fall of the Soviet Union, the lack of opportunities and resources available in the Armenian republic, especially in regards to education. In the second, the matter at hand is the perennial, existential tenuousness of never fully belonging in a host culture or nation as a member of the diaspora—an afterlife of the violent dispossession of Armenians at the fall of the Ottoman Empire. It is for these reasons that the movements of all four women, albeit in different directions, represent gestures against the colonial, national, and patriarchal drives to be rendered obscure, to be assimilated, or, with strong voices that speak/spoke in the name of justice, to be rendered silent.

The cyclicality and crisscrossing of these movements and encounters, then, is key: Avagyan and Aharonian meet because of the silence surrounding the works and lives of Kurghinian and Yesayan in the Armenian public and literary imaginations. As a result, Kurghinian and Yesayan would not be having a conversation in this untitled book if the Armenian canon had deemed them worthy of being properly archived, as their celebrated male counterparts have been. With a title that reflects an aporia that had gone unnamed for nearly a century, *Girq-anvernagir*, or *A Book, Untitled*, attempts to bring attention to the grammar of what was made to be nearly unspeakable, or, as Avagyan puts it, what was *deliberately made to disappear*. Indeed, it would take the imagination and drive of two women, whose own political subjectivities and voices were being structurally muffled, to ask the critical questions about the effects of censorship. Whether that censorship be patriarchal or governmental, they assert that it results in structural silence, often at the expense of women's and other socially minoritized people's voices, without critical accountability.

"Busts of all the beloved figures are arranged in the lobby of the state university. 'But where is she,' asks Lara. 'Why isn't her bust there?' / I answer," writes the unnamed narrator . . . "If we could have recovered all of the pages that had been torn out, burned, and destroyed by the critics, the libraries would simply overflow." How might the modern Armenian woman or feminist recognize herself through the history presented to her by a patriarchal society, which, according to Vahan Ishkhanyan in *Girq*'s Introduction (6), is a history of deception in which women's ideas of their emancipation in Armenia *were potentially* destroyed? Avagyan once recounted this story to me:

> I recall, during the final Soviet years in the 1980s, that in the textbook we had [there was] this ugly woman [Kurghinian]. I must have been in sixth or seventh grade . . . It was a very bad print, and yet she had my name, Shushanik, and she was born in 1876, a hundred years before me, and those were the only two things I remembered. We skipped over her and never read her literature. Many years later when I was trying to think, after reading so many other non-Armenian feminist writers . . . I asked myself, *Don't we have any feminists?*, and that's how Kurghinian's name came back to me. I started digging into her and I was very afraid I'd be disillusioned when I found out who she really was. But as I went into the museum and dug through her

notebooks I really realized she was a revolutionary writer for her time. I was researching Kurghinian, and I also knew about Zabel Yesayan and I was curious about her, but I didn't have the time, nor was I quite comfortable researching in Western Armenian. I'd contacted Lara about this book. At the time she was in Canada and I said that I wanted to publish a translation of Kurghinian, asking her if she knew of a good publisher or fund. She told me that she was coming to Armenia to research Zabel Yesayan, and that's how I found out about her interest . . . She moved to Armenia in about 2000, and my way of understanding Lara was through Yesayan. We would talk about Yesayan, I'd tell her about Kurghinian, and we'd compare and discuss and write . . . [and] our conversations paralleled with Yesayan and Kurghinian. (Avagyan and Cachoian, Interview, Yerevan/Istanbul, 2014)

If the legacies of Kurghinian and Yesayan had been disseminated instead of obscured, how might the narrative of the Armenian literary tradition in the twentieth century have been different? What form might the development of political and feminist thought, or literary aesthetics in an Armenian context, have taken had there been unobscured access to or the complete archival preservation of some of Armenian literature's most consequential writers?

Cameroonian philosopher Achille Mbembe's thoughts on the limits of the archive help us to, at the very least, better grasp what structures the roots of such fundamental frustrations. What we come to understand as "archives," explains Mbembe in "The Power of the Archive and Its Limits," are not constituted so much by the material documents or lack of them stored in an institution as much as by "the process which converts a certain number of documents into items *judged to be worthy of preserving*" (20, emphasis mine).

Archives, then, are not *just* about the documents or objects present, preserved, or altogether absent in an institution or holding cell of ostensible knowledge production. Instead, to speak about archives is to speak about "the exercise of a specific power and authority" that judges, discriminates, and selects, "granting a privileged status to certain written documents, and the refusal of that same status to others, thereby judged 'unarchivable'" (20), explains Mbembe in the same essay. If "the archive is not a piece of data, but a status," as Mbembe concludes, then Kurghinian and Yesayan—perhaps as socialist-leaning activists, or perhaps as talented wordsmiths and critically thinking women whose works stood out among their surrounding mediocrity—were deemed too dangerous to be worthy of holding it. Indeed, to have bestowed either writer their due status would have also meant to condone their vision of a world in which women's voices were equal to men's, or in which living in a diverse and multiethnic society where the acceptance of a person's humanity, regardless of their ethnoreligious background, was possible. But instead, Avagyan's novel opens with the first line of a letter addressed to Marina Tsvetaeva, the lines of which read, "When you love, you live without Hope."

Zabel Yesayan was already aware of the possibility of not being granted this privileged status—a warning passed down to her from none other than another feminist Armenian writer, Madame Srpouhi Dussap, when, as a young woman, Yesayan and her friends go to visit her in her parlor in Pera, Constantinople. "She told me," writes Yesayan in her memoir, "that in our day and age, a woman who wanted to carve out a place for herself in society was still not tolerated . . . To overcome all of these obstacles, I needed to exceed mediocrity." Yet Madame Dussap was wrong about one thing: it wasn't only imperative that Yesayan and other women writers exceed mediocrity in life, which Yesayan did impressively. She would also have to overcome the prejudices of those who came after her, who would inherit her writing, archive it, analyze it, handle it lovingly (or *ousoumna-SIREL*), and above all, maintain its status long after her death. The question of status and its censorship, then, is at the heart of Avagyan's literary experiment, and readers accompany her with it, sifting through fragments that have long been buried in the ruins of a destroyed plot.

"Literature is a weapon to struggle against injustice," wrote Zabel Yesayan. In Avagyan's response to the Armenian literary canon's diminishing and erasure of Shushanik Kurghinian and Zabel Yesayan, *Girq* takes Yesayan's task to arms by formally mimicking the very erasure and distortion of the canon that it criticizes. *Girq* announces its auto-censorship through the use of asterisks (or *****), plagiarizes poetry and prose (from Yesayan, Kurghinian, and others), and uncovers lost h(er) stories. In doing so, *Girq* enacts censorship and provokes the question of "who can author?" to echo the male-dominated, heteropatriarchal historiography to which it responds. This historiography has written the two revolutionary authors/ protagonists as domestic fixtures who've remained behind the closed doors of "tradition" and domestication, having been instrumentalized as Soviet propaganda and/or Armenian nationalism while largely ignoring their contribution to political, aesthetic, and feminist thought in the transnational Armenian milieu.

As such, with poetry by a series of authors who go unnamed, quoted sections of telegrams by Kurghinian and Yesayan that the typist/writer/translator and Lara discover in the dusty boxes of the state archives, Avagyan's scathing critique of the methods of erasure shared by literary critics, editors, and governmental regimes alike as she translates Kurghinian's poetry, and a series of unsent or unarrived love postcards to an unknown recipient, *Girq-anvernagir* is a translator's stream-of-consciousness novel. Indeed, through this elongated translator's note, the reader comes to learn not only the back stories of the writers that informed the urgency of Avagyan's translations, but also, about the typist/writer/translator herself and how those same heteropatriarchal methods of erasure are still enacted, against her and all of us, in the present.

"Intricately complicated, deliciously slippery: where to draw the line between the *life* and the *work*, between *theory* and *practice*?" writes literary theorist Alex Brostoff and art practitioner Lauren Fournier about the bourgeoning genre of autotheory in their introduction to "Autotheory ASAP! Academia, Decoloniality, and 'I'" in *ASAP/Journal* (2022, 489–502). Indeed, autotheory is an apt genre to describe a work that at once is a story of its protagonists as much as it is about the author herself and her relationship to those protagonists; a novel that, while telling its story, theorizes itself in its own telling; a novel in which the author, the narrator, and characters, slip, one into another. And like this—deconstructing hegemonic ways of knowing and understanding both History and the subject(s) who come to write it—Avagyan's novel is an encounter with how the personal structures our re-knowing of the social, "sutur[ing] self to social to structural, underscoring their emergence as mutually constitutive and interdependent," as Brostoff and Fournier continue.[3] As Avagyan once explained,

This book is a poem unlike any other poem, it is a novel unlike any other novel, it is a translator's note unlike any other translator's note, and it is a critical essay unlike any other critical essay. It is something in the process of becoming, it has not yet developed into any kind of genre, or it is a synthesis of genres—a text that bleeds into various categories and feeds on various realms like fact and fiction, and hence it refuses categorization. It can be anything—

(Avagyan and Cachoian, Interview, Yerevan/Istanbul, 2014)

Yet, through this weaving in and out of *Girq's* fragmented prose and its polyphony of voices, it is difficult at times to keep track of *who* is speaking, or whose words are being cited or appropriated. Several of *Girq's* chapters, for example, bear the names of Kurghinian's poems, yet they remain unmarked, and the reader is left to wonder who has authored these lines. Taking a rather socialist-feminist stance, the typist/writer/ translator suggests that the absence of quotation marks deprivatizes words, giving them over to a plurality of interpretations, narratives, and possibilities:

Sometimes, reader, the typist/writer forgets to put quotation marks around cited words or sentences. / Does that mean she steals others' words? / Which is worse: To let the living words of the poet die in damp boxes in dark, treacherous rooms or to sow them like seeds, mixed with another's words, to revive them and let them bloom in untitled fields? / Besides, quotation marks privatize words and make them someone else's property. / The words belong neither to the typist/writer nor to you, reader. / They simply unite our past, present, and future.

Indeed, such methods of decolonial citational practice have also been employed by other writers of autotheory whereby, from the perspective of the writer's embodied subjectivity in time and space—that is, the material and social conditions that make them them—their bodily experience helps us to think about and through high theory differently, not the other way around. In *Testo Junkie* (2013), for example, Paul B. Preciado directly takes the theories of various cultural philosophers to task *through* and *because* of the bodily transformations they undergo while on testosterone. In Preciado's case, the experience of the transitioning body pushes *theory* to think differently about itself, as well as to think differently about the body. Maggie Nelson's *The Argonauts* (2015) uses yet another kind of citational practice. While Nelson does not directly reference the theorists she quotes in the main body of the text —theorists and theories that lovingly accompany her into her new relationship with bodies while she is pregnant and her partner is transitioning—Nelson's citational kin are enacted as co-writers of her autobiographical novel, named in italics in the book's margins. They are not a part of the text, but are adjacent to it; and they are, nonetheless, named.

Avagyan's autotheoretical approach in the deliberate unnaming of her citational kin, then, is even more radical. In this citational iteration, unnaming or not citing at all (re)enacts a violence at the same time as it is didactic, gesturing towards a more socialist norm; it is also a way to pay tribute to the writers who have most influenced her; and in its final instance, perhaps it also displays Avagyan's own embodied frustration with the Armenian canon and its readers. It asks, *Why do you,* reader, so relentlessly want to know what belongs to whom; from where does that desire to possess such knowledge come; and finally, if you do happen to know its source, just how much more richly does this text arrive to you?

But still, aren't we at least curious to know which chapter titles are echoes of Kurghinian's poetry? Which poetic verses "belong" to Avagyan? Couldn't it be Avagyan's duty to fill us in? To tell us which words are Kurghinian's, which Yesayan's, which her own? And are there still others? Avagyan refuses to labor the answers to these questions for her readers. Instead, she challenges us to be archeologists along with her and ask, *Under which circumstances does one acquire the right to claim authorial voice? How does authorship invoke ownership, and how does ownership—based upon the concept of* possession—*reproduce (colonial and capitalist) hegemony?* "Any kind of writing is always a response to something else," says Avagyan.

Yet can we divest that power of ownership by just refusing to play by its rules and not cite authors? How might History and the archive also be privatized, effected and affected by that hegemonic patriarchal reproduction? As such, to what extent has History been edited and distorted, and thus what might a subversion of distortion *through* distortion look like?

In my own reading—as certainly one person's interpretation is never exhaustive or whole—four major narrative layers unfold to address these questions: the first, the presentation of the silenced archival traces of Kurghinian and Yesayan; the second, the reconnaissance work of the typist/writer/translator and Lara as they uncover the archive's violence in censoring material, and then their *imagining* of what could have been a conversation between Kurghinian and Yesayan (animating the gaps and silences of the archive beyond what its patriarchal contours might allow); the third, *Girq's* diary-entry type prose, reflecting on the censorship or editorial violence its author experiences as a translator, and which she parallels to the historical censorship of Kurghinian and Yesayan; and the fourth, the series of love postcards written in italics and addressed to an unknown recipient that reflect irreconcilable gaps and distance created by time, by language, and by space. *Indeed, while these postcards are here in the book, "saved from exile," some things, dear reader, just remain untranslatable.* Each of these layers contributes to Avagyan's commentary on erasure.

Enacting auto-censorship on her own text to reflect this violence, Avagyan performatively and provocatively parallels the historical censorship of her authors, beseeching her reader to question it:

> Anyway, reader, know that this book arrives to you incomplete. / In the lines you see the (*) mark, know that in these parts the most potent words from the original text have been removed. / Every book, especially a collection of translated poems, goes through a "cleansing" process. / For you, reader, because apparently the editors know (and know well) what you need, in what quantity and in what form.

Throughout *Girq*, the reader encounters strings of asterisks, marked omissions, and struck-through sentences. The historical "cleansing" processes to which the typist/writer/translator alludes above are the censored letters Yesayan wrote to her daughter, Sophie, while in prison. Though written ambiguously to guard against being seized and destroyed by the prison authorities, her letters were nonetheless inspected, "edited," and reappropriated by her Soviet "investigators" before they were sent. Still, readers might ask, is the typist/

writer/translator presenting us with "real" historical documents, or are these figments of her own imagination? In this juxtaposition of history with the present, Avagyan offers a biting commentary on the editing/publishing institution itself as being contaminated by market values in its conception of readers as consumers rather than questioners, ultimately leading to a text's contamination. "A lot of things are missing," she writes. "For example, two sentences from this chapter are missing. / The most important part is missing, but you, my good reader, don't notice it. / You don't ask questions." Thus, Avagyan provokes us to be active readers who dig through and challenge the layered silencings of and deviations from the past. And according to the typist/writer/translator, "you can't find the truth . . . unless you deviate . . ."

And thus, Avagyan presents us with a new kind of story, one that, in theory and in practice, connects the legacies of the past with stakes in the present. Still, that story does not dictate or define for us what those connections might be. "History," as Saidiya Hartman writes in her 2008 essay "Venus in Two Acts," "pledges to be faithful to the limits of fact, evidence, and archive" (9), yet we must remember, as explained by Mbembe earlier, that the archive is itself a result of an *edited* hegemonic narrative—one that has cherry-picked who gets represented in History, and how. Perhaps creative writing about archival material intensifies the fiction of History, decoupling us from the idea of history as fixed, or its archive as definitive.

Girq's creative project predates Hartman's similar concept of "critical fabulation" by two years, mixing archival research, theory, and creative writing to imagine how the disappeared will be re-membered back into history through interpretation. And while Hartman employs "critical fabulation" to imagine and *write in*, through fiction, what has been left out of or that remains irrecoverable from the colonial archives on the Middle Passage, Avagyan brings us East, to the regulatory forms of racialization and erasure in the Ottoman Empire, the Soviet Union, and still today in the nation-states that have inherited their legacies. As Avagyan suggests, then, this method of writing about archival aporias prompts readers each time to "re-find" more of what is concealed: "Someone will remember the disappeared, and while remembering, will write verses dedicated to them, and while reading those verses, yet another will re-remember them. / The loss of one thing will help re-find another." And the typist/writer/translator frames this writing-remembering process as inherently deviant: "A book that, throughout its creation, changes and distances itself from its original aim . . . Whatever's impossible to solve in reality, I'm trying at least to understand by writing."

As I confronted what translating *Girq* from one language to the next might mean for the book's project, I also participated in Avagyan's experiment of multi-authorship. If we can compare Avagyan's multi-voiced, multi-genre text to what Mikhail Bakhtin in "Discourse in the Novel" calls the heteroglossic imagination—when "another's speech in another's language . . . express(es) authorial intentions [through] refract[ion]" (324), then *translation* may also be a deviation that allows the translator to be an equal player in the creation of a new text—giving, as Benjamin famously wrote in "The Task of the Translator," the text an afterlife, or perhaps a new life altogether.

Avagyan's formal and thematic deviations encouraged me to follow in kind. Thus, deviation became the politics of my own translation of *Girq*. "To comprehend something new, one must learn another language, customs, culture; in a word, they must live another way of life," writes Avagyan. Yet, how to translate concepts into English that Avagyan has coined in Armenian (who said that Varoujan was the only master of neologisms in Armenian)? There are several, for example, in Chapter 15, "To the Square!" The first is *batsa-hayt(naber)el*: literally "open-seen/known(bring it forth)." Translation options included "extract(plain)," "dis-cover/un-cover/un-fold," and "dis(un)cover." What new and diverse meanings in English might each of these translation choices unfold? Avagyan herself once explained the term to me—a merging of the two words that share the same root: *batsahaytel* and *haytnaberel*—to discover and uncover, or extract and explain. The merger, however, aims to intensify the process of discovery, a type of "discovery through exposition . . ." In this moment of being lost *between* the translations, the loss of one thing might help to re-find another. The reader will find "dis(un)cover" as the final choice in this translation.

The second example from Chapter 15 is the separation of the compound word *ousoumnasirel* as *ousoumna-SIREL*. *Ousoumnasirel*, which means "to learn, study, read, examine," is a verb formed from the noun *ousoum*, meaning "study" or "education," and the verb *sirel*, meaning "to love." However, in Avagyan's text, the verb reads as *ousoumna-SIREL*, emphasizing the *love* of the process or to proceed *lovingly*. In the sentence, *ousoumna-SIREL* is used in the context of loving or being infatuated with the "learning" or "studying" of the roots of commonplace words in order to dis(un)cover new meanings within them. Indeed, at times I wondered if Avagyan's meta-critique laid in its challenge to (or almost *trolling* of) her future translator: find a proper translation for the very word that instructs you to go deep within it and find all the possibilities of its meaning. At least, this is what becomes clear in the process of translating such commonplace Armenian words, bringing them into a new language where they cannot be played with as comfortably as they can be in their native tongue. I hope to have accomplished, then, what Benjamin elegantly wrote of translation in "The Task of the Translator." "Instead of resembling the meaning of the original, [a translation] must *lovingly* and in detail incorporate the original's mode of signification, thus making both the original and the translation recognizable as fragments of a greater language" (69–82, emphasis mine, and to disclose some of Avagyan's own surreptitious citations).

After coming up with a plethora of possibilities, I settled on "exa-*mine*" as the translation of *ousoumna-SIREL*. In my opinion, the choice preserves the sense of studying or examining the roots of something, starting from the outside, or *exo-*, while italicizing *mine*, as in mining the roots of knowledge from the outside, in. Indeed, in my reading, it is the *love* of study that allows one to *mine* for knowledge . . . though it is important to remember that this interpretation is just that: merely mine.

Ultimately, reading *Girq* in English translation becomes an event through which a new language again calls upon Avagyan's reader to re-create words to re-create a story. Through the inherent deviation of translation itself, we are thus reminded of the aim of un-archiving in *Girq*: "Re-assume. Re-analyze. Re-remember," in order to ex-tract(plain) or "dis(un)cover."

Yet, what distinguishes deviation from invention and hypercorrection? The title of Chapter 20 is "*Anraqeloutyoun, kam Yeraznerov mi' tar snound*" ("**An**raqeloutyoun, or Don't Feed Me Dreams," boldface mine). The latter part of the sentence is taken from the title of a Kurghinian poem. But "*An-raqeloutyoun*" does not mean anything in Armenian. How to translate something also obscure in Armenian? Trying to make sense of the word, I first gravitated towards what *was* intelligible: the word began with "*an*," a prefix equivalent to "un-" or "in-" for negation in English. But what was the meaningless, abstract noun "*raqeloutyoun*" to which it was attached?

There was yet another option. Influenced by Avagyan's deviations and tendency for word play by inserting letters into words to break them apart and make a word that contained two or more words in one (like *batsa-hayt(naber)el* [dis(un)cover] discussed above), I became hyperaware of these instances. I imagined that the "*n*" could actually be the "foreign" addition to the entire word. *An*raqeloutyoun does not mean anything, but *Araqeloutyoun* does: it means "mission," or "apostolicism," from which the adjective *araqelakan* or "apostolic," as in the Armenian Apostolic Church, derives. Perhaps here is where the two ideas collapsed into one: a negating *an* + *ara-qeloutyoun* = *an*raqeloutyoun. The noun becomes abstract with its "*outyoun*" ending (the -ism, -ness, or -tion in English). Very clever, I thought. I rendered the following options: Inapostolicism; A-ᵃpostolicism (taking a hint from the math equations in Chapter 6); A-(a)postolicism. I consulted Shushan, only to have her correct/edit/(censor?) my own interpretation. Instead, she imposed her "original meaning" . . . or, better stated, her "intention." *Anraqeloutyoun* was simply the state of being "without Raquel"; thus, "Raquel-lessness."

Beyond what I could both imagine and conjure up in my attempt to stay true to the deviating spirit of her text, Avagyan was simply (or not), referring to someone named "Raquel." And so, deviations apparently risk a translator's hypercorrections, bringing the text in a direction even its author could not have imagined. We would do well to remember that all translation, indeed, is interpretation. Even in their effort to keep true to a text's spirit and the words on the page, even the most well-intentioned and attentive translator deviates from the original path. Such, then, is an example of when the editing process between *author* and *translator* can be, if possible and perhaps in the best of worlds, a *very useful* and *generative* collaboration. In any case, "the loss of one thing will help re-find another." Who are you, Raquel? How were you lost? Are you reading this text now? Could you read it before? Or are you only to be known by your inventor/rememberer? *Perhaps some things are not meant to be found . . .*

Due to the constraints and codes of the English language, in the manuscript's unedited version, I also gestured towards a certain opacity in my translation, which would have exposed my own political persuasions as a reader of *Girq*. Indeed, such is what I imagine as an autotheoretical praxis of translation—the moment in which, through the act of translation, the embodied subjectivity of the translator, which affects *how* the translator translates, becomes exposed. In this case, the translation of the ever-looming, gender-neutral third-person-singular pronoun, *na* (Eastern Armenian variant), also required deviation from the Armenian text. Mostly because of the text's fragmented character, which maintains its purposeful narratological ambiguity, *na*'s referent, oftentimes, is lost. Giving gender to *na* in any gender-ambiguous passage (and there are several) would have risked, in my opinion, writing an assumed gender-relationality (and sometimes either a hetero- or homo-, or queer-erotic timbre) into a scene. I was wholly uncommitted to making a choice between male or female gender pronouns in English. Indeed, each seemed inappropriate to me: either an overreading or underreading. And what's more, *assigning* a gender to *na* in these more ambiguous circumstances would mean writing out its ambiguity in the Armenian. In these moments, I wondered what kinds of possibilities a queer perspective on the translation of the ambiguous *na* offer?

While certain theories of translation seek to domesticate a text so that it does not, to use the Turkish saying, "smell like translation" (*çeviri kokuyor*), I wanted my translation to lean instead towards what I've called a praxis of "double" de-domestication. A translation practice of domestication seeks to make the translation appear as if it were not a translation but instead a product of the target language itself; indeed, as if it were written in it. This translation praxis was largely popular for centuries, yet contemporary critics beginning with Lawrence Venuti have critiqued such a practice as a colonization of the source text, disingenuously and inappropriately assimilating it. As such, Venuti famously proposes a translation theory against the domestication of a foreign text, so that the translation does not *pass* as a text "domestic" to its target language. Instead, Venuti proposes to preserve the "foreign" elements of the text in its translation. However, if the constraints of the target language foreclose these possibilities such that a text can be neither foreignized nor domesticated, this is not possible. Instead, a translation praxis of double de-domestication visibly estranges the text in English translation beyond the comfortable ambiguity of the Armenian, so that the translation becomes a renewed reading of the primary text, over, against, and beyond it. Indeed, as its Latin prefix suggests, *trans-* is not a state, but a process; not a return, but a movement *beyond*; a non-return that looks back on an "originary" object or place, changed. Sitting visibly in its ambiguity by refusing to pass or play by the rules of either-or, as a process of *throughness*, and whether about bodies of flesh or of text, *trans-* transforms. Thus, hoisting the translator into a position of hyper-visibility, double de-domestication is a second layer of textual foreignization caused by the constraints of the target language.

Instead of assigning gender to the *na*s in gender-ambiguous passages, I had originally chosen to *further* highlight the gender-ambiguity of the text beyond its original subtly by translating *na*, unless otherwise indicated, as "they." The use of they in the third-person singular (or in reference to a singular antecedent) is not new. Instead, it has a long history in the English language, dating back to at least the fourteenth century in written form, as described in "A brief history of singular 'they'" (2022) on the webpage of the Oxford English Dictionary. Today, the singular they has been re-adopted or put back into use as a pronoun used, the entry goes on to explain, "in cases where the gender of the antecedent . . . is unknown, irrelevant, or nonbinary, or where gender needs to be concealed." It is through this (presently queer) look to the past, then, that I chose to adopt the old form of the singular they; and this choice might be queer *only* in light of the queer or gender nonbinary community's recent adoption of it in order to be imagined otherwise and/or beyond the gender binary. But what's more, if I had instead chosen to inscribe the gender binary of "he" or "she" in my translation, I would have actually been distorting or censoring the queerly, strangely comfortable ambiguity of the Armenian in its use of the gender-neutral or gender-ambiguous singular, third-person pronoun *na*. The gender neutrality or ambiguity of Armenian plays a key function in Avagyan's text. For example, the book conveniently auto-censors or does not outwardly reveal its play with gender ambiguity in the love postcards. In my reading, this is purposeful: the postcards are quite aware that they do not reveal the gender of the recipient (or writer) to you, dear reader.

To be sure, the choice of the singular they would have revealed my own sociopolitical positionality, a Shklovskian "estranging" of the eighteenth-century conformity of English grammar, interjecting what in today's lexical field would be read as a queer framework of gender-ambiguous or non-binary possibility. As the English translator of Shklovsky from Russian, Avagyan's writing has been influenced by his work, which has also come to inform her own translation praxis and her politics of creating neologisms in Armenian. And so, while her translator's choice of singular they would have brought the text away from its own subtle ambiguities, in my opinion, it would have also opened it up to new readings beyond what the primary text might immediately offer. Perhaps too, this praxis would have remained in the spirit of Avagyan's project: "You can't find the truth, Lara, unless you deviate." *However, reader, remember these lines quoted above, and when you arrive to Avagyan's penultimate chapter,* "know that this book arrives to you incomplete . . . Every book, especially a collection of translated poems, goes through a 'cleansing' process. For you, reader, because apparently the editors know (and know well) what you need, in what quantity and in what form."

In the end, the singular they was nixed in most instances, and we (Shushan and I) have amicably and collectively chosen here to render in English what the author intended while writing, most specifically in the cases when there was a particular referent in the passage to whom it was necessary to refer by gender in order to maintain the continuity in the text and/or the reader's comprehension of the characters; these are the types of moments when both practical and ethical decisions are made between author and translator. Indeed, even though Barthes inaugurates the poststructuralist turn with his claim that "the author is dead," in most cases when translating contemporary literature, the elephant in the room is that the author is still speaking.

This time—not for the reader or the translator but for the writer herself—the English translation has opened up a new possibility of expression. *But just remember, dear English reader, that for the reader in Armenian, gender is still slippery; its ambiguity still exists.* In perhaps an ironic twist of its translator's initial intentions to make it queer and visibly strange in the English while Avagyan preferred to assign the pronouns in English that she'd initially imaged for her characters, even the author herself cannot escape it: *In the Armenian, gender is still pleasantly up for grabs.*

Through the questions it poses on authorship, censorship, and plagiarism, *Girq's* deviations demonstrate how literature written in Armenian can also question the Western-born neoliberal market's effects on aesthetic practice. The novel queries into the potential merits that a different political system —a socialist-feminist one, perhaps, based more on collectivity and polyphony than individualist or liberal "democracies"— might have. As Barthes claims with "The Death of the Author," the text writes him. There is no ownership *over* the text; to the contrary, it is the text—master of one—that reigns over its readers.

And yet where might we draw the line between a translator's interpretation versus their distortion? Is it not limiting to understand the act of translation as either a text's "legitimate" interpretation versus its distortion? And so, what if, in lieu of distortion, deviation provided renewed possibilities for translation? My English translation of *Girq-anvernagir* does not seek to domesticate the text. I chose to translate more literally, or rather, more closely to the Armenian rather than privilege language that might "flow better" in English so as to preserve the particularities of an Armenian-language mentality. Instead of Avagyan's repeated declarations throughout the novel that it has four authors, now in its English translation, it has five. Indeed, that "[t]he book has four—or five?—authors who are as different as the seasons of the year" (Chapter 22), is my own addition/deviation from the original content of the text as written in the Armenian. *It is also my way, reader, to remind you of the many interpretations through which this text arrives to you, not least of all your own.*

Inevitably, the choice to not wear the mask of the original may distance my audience. Is it also injustice? I have left some idioms more literally rendered to give the sense of the text's foreignness, attempting to preserve, as much as one can in a foreign tongue, the book's cultural milieu. As per Lawrence Venuti's estimation in *The Translator's Invisibility*, this choice is "rather to develop a theory and practice of translation that resists dominant target-language cultural values so as to signify the linguistic and cultural difference of the foreign text." Like Avagyan resists hegemonic gender hierarchy and national canon and history making, as her translator, and as someone aware of the inherent problematics or contradictions of translation into the colonial lingua franca of the globalized world, my intention is not to colonize or domesticate this story into one that can be easily translated to an English-speaking context. Instead, I hope this translation inevitably highlights the richness of Avagyan's prose, as well as the strangeness and deepened, unanticipated intimacies across global contexts that the Armenian language might bring to English, and vice versa.

One of these inherent strangenesses or unanticipated intimacies may be, for some English-language readers, the use of "black" in the text. Of *Book*'s narrator—possibly the author —it is written in defiant reclamation, "you're too irregular and black," or as Kurghinian writes of herself ambivalently in the poem "We As Two Separate Planets": "I, a black and somber exile." Echoing Kurghinian, Avagyan nods to the regimes of racialization to which Armenians were, and still are, subjugated, not just in Armenia and in Armenians' greater ancestral geographies, but also in Russia proper, where Kurghinian became a political refugee, forcing herself into exile in Rostov-on-Don. Extending well beyond the Western colonial world, the material-discursive regimes in course that subjugated Armenians in the (Russian) imperial, Soviet, and postcolonial contexts also function(ed) through the language of blackness and the ideological black(ening) of bodies.[4] In this context, blackness describes not just the somatic differences between "white," "blonde," and "luminous" Russians and the "dark-skinned," "dark-haired," "black" or "black-smeared" (*chernomazy*, among other more derogatory terms in Russian) Armenians of the South Caucasus, but it also describes Armenians' becoming Other by law and by language in their own lands. Such optical regimes served the advancement of the colonial discourse regarding "illuminated" Russians versus the peoples of the Caucasus who were (in) "dark(ness)" and thus in need of enlightenment. Kurghinian, as a result of her socialist activities, effectively became a "black exile" (or as she disaffectedly terms in Armenian, *sev njdeh*) in response to that colonization. In her writings both published and unpublished, Kurghinian vehemently claims "black" as the term of her otherness. A century later, Avagyan follows suit, but reclaims the term: "my little black darling[s]," or the other Othered-Armenian readers today who might be considered Kurghinian's kin and who can dare to imagine their empowerment as "black exiles"—or conceptual refugees—otherwise. With references to this particular regime of blackness that subtly pepper the text yet still arrive as powerfully acerbic, *Book*, perhaps unexpectedly, invites the English-language reader to examine how diverse regimes of racialization that employ blackness as their means of subjugation traffic on a wider global stage.

A Book, Untitled, with its formal, historical, and thematic deviations, and its many (women) authors—including its translator (the fifth!)—views writing and history as belonging to readers and their interpretations instead of as the sole product of the author, historian, editor, translator, or publishing house. It also illustrates what the process of truly collaborative work can open up for the reader. For readers of Armenian literary works, both old and new, I hope this translation arrives to you as an exciting gateway through which to engage with intertextual and radical prose from the Armenian republic. I hope it also acts as a lens through which to better understand some of the terms that animate this region of the South Caucasus, ex-Soviet republics, and diasporas of the Ottoman Empire and Middle East: as a transnation, Armenia straddles—and disrupts—all these categories.

A Book, Untitled and others like it still untranslated from the Armenian, both Eastern and Western, have much to share about how contemporary artists and authors understand and critique society, the particular and localized hegemonic paradigms of the history that has inscribed them, and the particular forms of gender hierarchy, nation-state aspirations, and ethnoracialized nationalisms in the post-Ottoman, post-Soviet, and diasporic contexts to and through which they respond. If there is a past to be honored, it can only be rendered more significant through the continued attention we give to contemporary works lest they, like Kurghinian and Yesayan, also be rendered insignificant.

Avagyan's project is careful not to re-prescribe the legacies of Kurghinian and Yesayan, but to remind us of our possibility to un-fix them from their archival stagnation: to see just how much *one small* archival opening can disrupt the resolute foundation of patriarchal history-making. In this way, reading *Girq-anvernagir* through the lens of queer or postcolonial theory might guide us in reading its challenges not as a dismantling of History so much as a provocation of the possibilities of the archive and history if they are stretched and expanded beyond their fixed, past-oriented foci.

I asked Shushan once why she hadn't written her book in English instead of Armenian, being that she'd lived in the United States for such a long time, had translated Shushanik Kurghinian's poetry and Viktor Shklovsky's prose, and so most certainly could have accessed a global readership for *Girq*. Her reply: The recovery of the interrupted connection could have only taken place in the mother tongue of these women—the typist/writer/translator—Lara—Kurghinian—Yesayan. Indeed, we might do well, as readers in the colonial language par excellence, to take stock of this pronouncement.

Handing that book, with its red and white cover, to me on that fall evening in Yerevan—a queer act of kinship and care through intimacies begun in disparate geographies and junctures—that small note in English was my nudge to get back to Venice and *learn them* something anew. As for the book, leaving us with open provocations instead of hermetic answers, *Girq* pushes us not only to ask, What else remains? but also, How might each new excavation, in a new language, herald another plethora of discoveries, alternate readings, and other possibilities for new aesthetic, social, and political paradigms? I can't wait to discover what possibilities await.

---

* A version of this afterword appeared as an essay by the same name in the *Queering Armenian Studies* special issue of the *Armenian Review*, 56:1–2, 2018.

1. The first iteration of this translation was made upon my return to l'Università Ca' Foscari Venezia, under the tutelage of Sona Haroutyunian, my second mentor there who, unconvinced of said mediocrity, both encouraged and made this translation possible.

2. At the time of its publication in 2006, *Girq-anvernagir* was one of the few published books that explicitly focused on the literary legacies of Shushanik Kurghinian and Zabel Yesayan (especially in a work of creative writing). After Marc Nichanian's *Writers of Disaster* (2002), Victoria Rowe's 2003 *A History of Armenian Women's Writing, 1880–1922*, Avagyan's 2005 publication of *I Want to Live: Poems of Shushanik Kurghinian* by AIWA Press, Melissa Bilal and Lerna Ekmekçioğlu's 2006 compilation *Bir Adalet Feryadı: Osmanlı'dan Türkiye'ye Beş Ermeni Feminist Yazar (1862–1933)*] (Istanbul: Aras Publishing), Lara Aharonian and Talin Suciyan's 2008 documentary film *Finding Zabel Yesayan*, and Jennifer Manoukian's 2014 translation of Yesayan's *The Gardens of Silihdar*, the floodgates have been opened to a renewed interest in the publication of Armenian women's writing by translators and scholars.

3. In the special issue of *ASAP/Journal* dedicated to autotheory, Alex Brostoff and Lauren Fournier describe what they understand as the bourgeoning genre of autotheory. I quote here at length as I find it integral to a reading of Avagyan's work: "Fusing self-representation with philosophy and critical theory, autotheory moves between 'theory' and 'practice,' between 'living,' 'thinking,' and 'making.' It is critical and it is creative; it is experiential and experimental; it is scholarly, and it is popular. It brings theory to life and life to theory. It plays with personal polemic, positing a speaking self in the

act of writing 'I,' and then, self-reflectively and self-reflexively, it deconstructs itself. Autotheory's genealogies spring from the institutions it seeks to critique. It privileges thinking *with* over thinking *against*; its politics of citation unveil its relations" (490).

4. The racialization of Armenians in the Ottoman and post-Ottoman imperial contexts—one which was subsequently exported into Western diasporic contexts—functioned through a different set of racialized vocabularies and structures. In the Ottoman context, Armenians attempted to incorporate themselves into Western colonial models of "whiteness" (as opposed to their corollary of "blackness" and being Muslim) in order to mark themselves as potentially worthy of being saved by Western Christian nations (with "whiteness" and Christianity as intimately linked) from the ethnic-cleansing campaigns against Armenians and other ethnoreligious/racial minorities by the late-Ottoman regime. For Armenians, their racialization in their ancestral lands west of the Arax River ultimately culminated in genocide in 1915.

CHAPTER GUIDES*

Woven in fragments, **Chapter 1, "Preface, or We as Two Separate Planets"** *(bearing a line from Kurghinian's 1908 poem "We as Two Separate Planets"), presents interspersed and unidentified voices that will be heard throughout the novel. It introduces lines from letters written from prison by Zabel Yesayan to her daughter Sophie, as well as the conversation between Avagyan and her friend Lara, who are contemporaneously searching for the lost legacies of the feminist writers Shushanik Kurghinian and Zabel Yesayan. The unidentified first person "I" is the narrator, who makes reference to a number of writers, works, historical figures, and legends, including: Zabel Yesayan's works* In the Waiting Room *and* Barpa Khachik; *Lavrenty Beria, chief of the Soviet security and secret police under Joseph Stalin; the Armenian legend of Akhtamar, the source of "Tamar's lamp";* Ringing of the Dawn, *Kurghinian's first and only published volume of poetry; the Arlez of Semiramis, stemming from Zoroastrian and Armenian myth; and Mount Ararat, the mountain that overlooks the city of Yerevan just beyond the Armenian–Turkish border.*

---

* The chapter guides stand in lieu of footnotes, and serve both as a list of citations and to further acquaint readers with the characters or places mentioned throughout the given chapter.

Chapter 1.5, "Letter to Violet," *is written in two tenses. In the present tense, the narrator reflects on her time waiting in the airport with her friend Tina as they discuss their previous days in Cape Cod. The past tense narrates the days prior, spent editing a translation manuscript of Shushanik Kurghinian's poetry with a group of women. This chapter begins* A Book, Untitled*'s ongoing commentary on translation and starts to present lines from the archival material being discovered by the typist/writer and Lara. Various lines of Kurghinian's poetry are dispersed throughout the chapter. Some are quoted, others not, and the narrator uses them both to envision her own alternative society, as well as begin the biographical story of Kurghinian's failed marriage. This chapter refers to the Armenian region of Zangezur; Lev Nikolaevich, or Tolstoy; contemporary artist Tina Bastajian (b. 1962) and contemporary writer Violet Grigoryan (b. 1962)—one of the founders and editors of the Armenian literary journal* Inknagir.*

In **Chapter 2, "Coming from Our Native Land . . ."** *(a line from Kurghinian's 1907 poem "To Avetik Isahakyan"), the narrator presents some of the personal notes that she has uncovered in Kurghinian's archive. The chapter recreates Kurghinian's first meeting with her husband Arshak and mentions the time Kurghinian spent in a health sanitorium. The figures of the narrator and Kurghinian begin to blur into each other. The chapter makes reference to Arkadii Dragomoshchenko (1946–2012), the foremost writer of Language Poetry in contemporary Russian literature and author of* Xenia; *Avetik Isahakyan (1875–1957), prominent Armenian lyric poet, writer, and public activist; and Nevsky Prospect, the main avenue in the city of St. Petersburg, Russia. The word used for "native land" in the chapter's title is the Armenian transliteration of "vatan," the Turkish form of the Arabic "watan," meaning homeland, country, or nation.*

In **Chapter 3, "A Distant Sorrow in the Flower-Garden of My Soul"** *(another line from a Kurghinian poem), Kurghinian and Yesayan meet at a café and begin to reflect on the heteropatriarchal canons of their times. Considered political dissidents by the Tsar's and Young Turk regimes, each recount how they escaped from their hometowns. In fragments, Kurghinian describes her trip to Russia, while Yesayan shares scenes she'd witnessed during the Hamidian massacres (1890s) and the Armenian Genocide (1915–23). The chapter references several Armenian intellectuals: literary and art critic Garegin Levonyan (1872–1947); writer, educator, and political activist Roupen Zartarian (1874–1915), and the famed lyric poets Daniel Varoujan (1884–1915) and Siamanto (Atom Yarjanian) (1878–1915), most of whom were murdered during the genocide. "Bolis" is the abbreviated form of "Gonsdandinobolis" or Constantinople. Armenians still refer to the city of Istanbul by this name.*

Chapter 4, "How I Write and How I Would Like to Write" *is a meditation—of the typist/writer, of the author, of Kurghinian, of Yesayan?—on writing. The chapter refers to Marina Tsvetaeva (1892–1941), a Moscow-born Russian/Soviet poet renowned for her poetry, verse plays, and prose, and with whom the first chapter of this book opens; Russian Jewish poet and essayist Osip Mandelstam (1891–1938), one of the "foremost members" of the Acmeist school of poets; and Violet Grigoryan (listed also in Chapter 1.5). The title of this chapter is borrowed from a 1934 essay by Zabel Yesayan of the same name, which uses "or" instead of Avagyan's change to "and."*

Chapter 5, "She's My Laurel and the Mighty Marble Statue of My Glory" *(another line from Kurghinian's poetry) takes place along different temporalities and voices. Shushanik Kurghinian describes her first day of school (recounted in her unpublished autobiography), and* *refers to the "Kirigan," most likely a nonstandard pronunciation of "Keragan"—an alphabet primer infused with religious teachings for schoolchildren. The chapter also refers to the Russian poet Valery Bryusov (1873–1924), for whom the Yerevan State Linguistic University is named; the contemporary Armenian literary scholars, poet, and translator Diana Der-Hovanessian (1934–2018) and Victoria Rowe, who wrote the introduction for Avagyan's translation of a collection of Kurghinian's poems (I Want to Live); and contemporary American author Micheline A. Marcom (b. 1968).*

Chapter 6, "The Inevitable Will Crown Us with an Inseparable Connection" *(a line from Kurghinian's 1909 poem "To Death"), in large part, presents an imagined conversation between Zabel Yesayan and the "interrogators" of the Soviet regime who imprisoned her during the Great Purge. The chapter makes reference to Kurghinian's poem "Nightfall" (translated by Avagyan), Vahan Totovents (1889–1938), Armenian writer, poet, and public activist from Turkish Armenia, who expatriated to Soviet Armenia and was also killed in Stalin's purge; Mariam Khatisyan (1845–1914), author, cultural activist, and president of the Armenian Women's Charity Union of Tiflis; and Sibil, the penname of Zabel Khanjian Asadour (1863–1934), Ottoman Armenian poet, writer, educator, publisher, and philanthropist.*

Chapter 7, "My Dear Sister, on The Occasion of Your Return" *(a line from Kurghinian's 1917 poem "Return" that reappears in the final chapter of the book), is a meditation on the city of Yerevan, fragmented with Kurghinian's and Yesayan's meeting and the continuation of Yesayan's interrogation. The chapter begins to blur the boundaries between historic and literary canons, and their censorship by the hegemonic structures of power to which they were subjected. To this end, the Soviet interrogators are given hypothetical names, which happen to* *be, instead of Soviet officials, the Armenian literary figures Nshan Beshiktashlian (1898–1972), the Ottoman Armenian writer who'd settled in Paris, and Gostan Zarian (1885–1969), Armenian intellectual and lyric writer from Ottoman Turkey—both of whom somehow survived the Genocide. The woman with a walking stick refers to Shushanik Kurghinian, who had a limp and used a cane; "Yeritasardakan" (meaning "youth") is the metro stop next to Yerevan State University.*

Chapter 8, "But Only One Bright Ray? . . . Oh, That's Not Enough, Dear Gentlemen" (a line from Kurghinian's 1905 poem "My Song"), references Kurghinian's time in the hospital due to gout. The typist/writer/translator figure is introduced here; finally, French Armenian philosopher and literary critic Marc Nichanian is mentioned, whose letter to the author will appear in Chapter 13.

In Chapter 9, "There Are Unknown Songs . . . Silent and Voiceless" (a line from Kurghinian's 1908 poem "There Are Songs"), one of the interrogators takes interest in Yesayan's writing while he discusses Charlotte Brontë's Jane Eyre. *The interrogators threaten to transfer Yesayan to Leninakan, the name given during the Soviet period to Gyumri (Kurghinian's Alexandrapol), the second largest city in Armenia.*

Chapter 10, "Reversal, or Peripety" features Kurghinian's play The Solitary Woman *(1914) and excerpts Zabel Yesayan's memoir* The Gardens of Silihdar *(1935). All Avagyan's direct quotes from the original* Silihdari Bardeznere *(The Gardens of Silihdar) are rendered here in English through Jennifer Manoukian's 2014 translation of the memoir. The excerpt quoted from the memoir in this chapter recounts Yesayan and her friends' visit to the famed Ottoman Armenian feminist writer Srpouhi Dussap in her parlor in Pera—a neighborhood* on the European side of Istanbul known for its community of artists and intellectuals. The chapter also references Kurghinian's poem "On the River Don" (1907).

Chapter 11, "That's Her, They Say, the Poet" *(the title of a Kurghinian poem written in 1907), discusses the poems of Shushanik Kurghinian. Throughout the chapter, there is both quoted and unquoted material written by the literary critic Hovhanness Ghazaryan, Kurghinian's biographer who wrote a monograph on her that was published in 1955. The end of the chapter consists of a letter to Berj (short for Berjouhi), a curator in the archive library at the Museum of Literature and Art where Avagyan went to research the lives of Kurghinian and Yesayan.*

Chapter 12, "A Short Chapter," *is an imagined reflection by Yesayan on the death of her friend, the writer Vahan Totovents, written from her prison cell. "Areni" refers to a type of Armenian sweet or dry red wine that is produced in a village of the same name, in the province of Vayots Dzor in the Armenian republic; lavash is a type of circular, thin flat bread made throughout the Caucasus and the Middle East, and is baked on the inside wall of a tonir, a large underground ceramic vase; Shirak is one of the provinces of Armenia; finally, the Feast of the Holy Translators refers to the holiday in the Armenian Apostolic Church that celebrates the literary figures and saints who founded the Armenian alphabet, translated the Bible, and began a movement to translate important literary works into the Armenian language in the fifth century.*

Chapter 13, "They Told Me" *(the title of a 1905 Kurghinian poem), features a letter to the author from Marc Nichanian (see notes to Chapter 8) responding to Avagyan's request to review her transla-*

tions of Kurghinian's poems and write a line to be included on the back cover of the publication. Nichanian writes about the censored legacy of Shushanik Kurghinian.

Chapter 14, "We Happened Upon Each Other Again in a Room, Me and the Sweet-Tongued Poet of the Wood" (a line from Kurghinian's 1908 poem "We Happened Upon Each Other Near a Rose Bush"), refers to the Goshavank Monastery, located in present day Armenia, and named after the thirteenth-century monk and legal scholar Mkhitar Gosh; Vahan Teryan (1885-1920), Armenian poet and public activist; and the 2003 novel by Armenian writer Karén Karslyan, X Frames/Second.

Chapter 15, "To the Square!" refers to Hrant Yesayan, Zabel Yesayan's son, who visits her in prison; a khachkar, or cross-stone, is an ancient Armenian artform dating back to early Armenian Christianity, and likely a tradition adopted from pagan times. The khachkar is specific to Armenian religious art, in which crosses are carved from a single stone with intricate lattice work and several depths, all holding significance; Mesrop Mashtots (d. 440) was an Armenian theologian (later canonized), linguist, and hymnologist who created the Armenian alphabet in 405 in order to translate the Bible from Greek.

Chapter 16, "An Unbearable Chapter," makes reference to Tolstoy's "Arzamasian terror," the famous dream of Tolstoy that renders him forever cognizant of the inescapability of his own death; Maid of Orléans, also known as Joan of Arc; Shushanik der Marderosian, the mother of Vosdanig Manoog Adoian—the birth name of the Armenian American abstract expressionist painter Arshile Gorky. Adoian's mother is featured in the famous painting The Artist and His

Mother *(1936), which is the artist's decade-long product of a memory piece related to the Armenian Genocide.*

Chapter 17, "No New Armenian Writer Has Inspired Me." *Throughout this chapter, the narrator directly quotes or references poems written by Kurghinian, some of which Avagyan translated and published in* I Want to Live: Poems of Shushanik Kurghinian *(2005). In this present translation of* A Book, Untitled, *the translators of Kurghinian's poems are left ambiguous. The poems which were translated by Avagyan are re-used here; otherwise, all other translations are by this translator/author. The specific translator has not been indicated. Nietzsche's* Zarathustra *and Aeschylus, the father of Greek tragedy, are also mentioned.*

Chapter 18, "There Was No Water in the Desert I Crossed" *also bears the lines of another Kurghinian poem. The narrator refers to Scutari, modern day Üsküdar, a neighborhood on the Anatolian side of Istanbul, Turkey. The Marmara Sea touches the southern banks of Istanbul, connected to the Black Sea through the Bosporus Strait. Again, the English-language rendering of Yesayan's memoir is from Manoukian's translation.*

Chapter 19, "At Dawn" *(the title of a 1906 Kurghinian poem). This chapter references Tiflis, the local name for Tbilisi, the capital of Georgia; Alexandrapol was the name used between 1837 and 1924 to refer to Gyumri, the second largest city in modern day Armenia. The city was originally referred to as Kumayri, then Gyumri, Alexandrapol during the tsarist reign, Leninakan under the USSR (1924– 1990), and then again as Gyumri. It was Shushanik Kurghinian's hometown. The term* jan *is used in one of Arshak Kurghinian's letters. Arriving from the Persian meaning "body, soul, life," the term is* *also used in Armenian, Kurdish, and Turkish as a term of endearment meaning "dear, life, soul."*

Chapter 20 is entitled **"Raquellessness, or Don't Feed Me Dreams."** *"Don't feed me dreams" is a line taken from a Kurghinian poem. The* tar *and* saz *are traditional string instruments of Anatolia; a* bayati *is the name of a musical node in systems of music across the Levant, and corresponds to the natural minor scale with a half-flat second degree, with the scale's dominance on the fourth degree; Hafiz, Shiraz, Sayat-Nova, and Jivani refer to regional Persian, Caucasian, and Armenian bards; the Narek refers to the Armenian Book of Lamentations written by the Armenian saint, Gregory of Narek. It is one of the most important prayer books of the Armenian church. "Going to the people," mentioned in Kurghinian's play, is a reference to the populist movement in the Russian Empire in 1874.*

Chapter 21, "Take Away My Longing for Our Native Land," *is a line from Kurghinian's poem "To Avetik Isahakyan." The chapter makes reference to* tufa, *a type of soft limestone commonly found near bodies of water. It is a common material used in the construction of buildings and Armenian churches in the Caucasus, where it is pink in color. As in Chapter 2, the Turkish term* vatan *for homeland, or native land, is used in the chapter title. Vera Hakobyan was a famous voice on the Armenian Public Radio from the early 1950s till the end of the Soviet era. Akhtamar is a local Armenian cigarette brand. Bakzal refers to a character in one of Karén Karslyan's books.*

Chapter 22, "On Black Nights When There Are No Stars" *(a line from Kurghinian's 1908 poem "I Wish"), refers to the city of Van, a former Armenian province of Western Armenia located in Eastern Anatolia.*

Chapter 23, "I'll Wander and Endure . . ." (a partial line from Kurghinian's 1907 poem "I Want to Live"), is a meditation on the work and legacy of Shushanik Kurghinian. The chapter addresses the theme of sex work in Kurghinian's poetry—a major theme throughout the nineteenth century.

Chapter 24, "And They Swung from the Infamous Gallows of the Dark Prisons" (another line from a Kurghinian poem) refers to several songs in the album Listen to My Heart, sung by the contemporary singer Datevik Hovanesian. The Vernissage refers to an open-air artisan and antique market in Yerevan. A dragon-carpet, or vishapagorg, is a uniquely Armenian style of carpet weaving from the South Caucasus.

In **Chapter 25, "Some Blackguards . . . Proudly Pinned Down . . . My Invincible Wing"** (another line from a Kurghinian poem), Avagyan refers to Yeghishe Charents (1897–1937), a famous Eastern Armenian poet; Alexander Tamanian was the architect and city planner of the modern city of Yerevan, designed in a circle based on the urban design of Paris; Marietta Shahinyan (known as Shaginyan in the English-speaking world) (1888–1982) was an Armenian Soviet writer and activist, who became famous as a communist writer experimenting in satirico-fantastic fiction. "Dzorages"—a Soviet term for the hydro station located in the Dzoragyugh village of the Lori region of Armenia—is also the location in which Shahinyan's novel Gidrotsentral is based.

Chapter 26, "Conclusion, or 'Return' to the Beginning," refers to "Return," the title of a 1917 poem by Kurghinian.

Cover art and design: Amandine Forest

Art Direction: Tice Cin, Kristen Vida Alfaro

Typesetting and E-book production: Abbas Jaffary

Editor: Tatiana Ryckman

Copyeditor: David McNamara, Emily Roberts

Proofreader: Mayada Ibrahim

Acquiring Editor: Kristen Vida Alfaro

Publishing Assistant: Nguyễn Đỗ Phương Anh

Publicist: Inara Iskandar

Marketing Manager: Trà My Hickin

Rights Director: Julia Sanches

Publisher: Kristen Vida Alfaro

Made with Hederis

Printed and bound by Clays Ltd, Elcograf S.p.A.

ABOUT TILTED AXIS PRESS

Tilted Axis publishes mainly work by Asian and African writers, translated into a variety of Englishes. This is an artistic project, for the benefit of readers who would not otherwise have access to the work – including ourselves. We publish what we find personally compelling.

Founded in 2015, we are based in the UK, a state whose former and current imperialism severely impacts writers in the majority world. This position, and those of our individual members, informs our practice, which is also an ongoing exploration into alternatives – to the hierarchisation of certain languages and forms, including forms of translation; to the monoculture of globalisation; to cultural, narrative, and visual stereotypes; to the commercialisation and celebrification of literature and literary translation.

We value the work of translation and translators through fair, transparent pay, public acknowledgement, and respectful communication. We are dedicated to improving access to the industry, through translator mentorships, paid publishing internships, open calls and guest curation.

Our publishing is a work in progress – we are always open to feedback, including constructive criticism, and suggestions for collaborations. We are particularly keen to connect with Black and indigenous translators of Asian and African languages.

tiltedaxispress.com
@TiltedAxisPress